F
MOR

Morrison, Dorothy

Whisper again

Books by Dorothy Nafus Morrison

BIOGRAPHIES:

LADIES WERE NOT EXPECTED
Abigail Scott Duniway and Women's Rights

CHIEF SARAH
Sarah Winnemucca's Fight for Indian Rights

UNDER A STRONG WIND
The Adventures of Jessie Benton Fremont

FICTION:

WHISPER, GOODBYE

SOMEBODY'S HORSE

WHISPER AGAIN

Whisper Again

Whisper Again

Dorothy Nafus Morrison

ATHENEUM   1987   New York

Atheneum
Macmillan Publishing Company
866 Third Avenue, New York, NY 10022
Collier Macmillan Canada, Inc.

Type set by Haddon Craftsmen, Allentown, Pennsylvania
Printed and bound by Fairfield Graphics, Fairfield, Pennsylvania
Designed by Jean Krulis
First Edition

10 9 8 7 6 5 4 3 2 1

Library of Congress Cataloging-in-Publication Data

Morrison, Dorothy N.
Whisper again.

Summary: When, in an effort to raise money, her
parents lease part of their ranch to a children's camp,
thirteen-year-old Stacey is positive that she can never
accept the intrusion of strangers in all her favorite
places.
[1. Ranch life—Fiction. 2. Camps—Fiction.
3. Horses—Fiction] I. Title.
PZ7.M8293Wg   1987   [Fic]   87-924
ISBN 0-689-31348-9

To David, Fiona, & Alan Carl

Contents

Whisper Again

1.
They're Here!

*This was the Absolutely Worst
Day of my entire life.*
—STACEY'S DIARY
JUNE 17

"THEY'RE HERE! STACEY! COME *quick*!" Michelle's voice
rose to a shriek as she flung open the barn door, letting
in a burst of sunshine. It was mid-June in the Oregon
ranch country, and the air was warm, sharp with sage.
"The bus just turned into the lane! It looks like a school
bus, only it's red." She thudded down the aisle, and
Brandy, their golden shepherd-collie, jumped to his feet
with one ear cocked.

Thirteen-year-old Stacey Chambers, who had been
brushing out the corners of a manger, peered over the stall
door. "Really, Mish, do you always have to *pound*?" she
said. "I thought some elephants, at the very least, were
coming in. Can't you remember that. . . ."

"I know! We have to tippytoe because Breeze is a *baby*. The only foal in the whole wide world that ever lost its *mother.*" Michelle rattled the door latch. "You don't mind a little noise, do you, Funny-guy? Anyway, you might as well get used to it. There are going to be lots of people around from now on."

Drawing a long sigh, Stacey reminded herself that Michelle was only nine. But—couldn't she, just once, *walk* instead of—of—gallumphing? Couldn't she, just once, keep her voice down? Especially now, when Breeze was so young and had almost died along with his mother? Most especially *today*? Just thinking about that bus made Stacey want to rush outside and shake her fist at the sky and howl.

Michelle, however, was laughing. "Look at him, Stace! He's so *cute!*" She slipped into the stall while Brandy, with a weighty sigh, flopped down again, his chin on his paws.

Stacey glanced at Breeze. Shiny black, he was standing close to Mr. Lee, the kind, poky, twenty-one-year-old gelding who kept him company. When Stacey held out her hand, Mr. Lee lumbered forward to nuzzle her palm. "Nice old fellow," she murmured. "You're trying to be a good mama. Are you tired of being shut up in the barn?"

"Of course he is!" exclaimed Michelle. "And I'm tired of hanging around here, too. Hurry *up*! I told you, the bus has *come*!"

"You go ahead." Stacey turned back to the manger

just as several loud thumps resounded from the adjoining stall. "I hear you, Beautiful," she called out. "Be patient a minute more." She smiled. "Listen, Mish . . . Whisper's pounding again! She knows—anyway, she hopes—I have an apple for her. But I've got to get this manger cleaned up first, so the dust won't blow up Mr. Lee's nose and give him pneumonia, or emphysema, or something. He's snuffling worse all the time."

"Oh, sure—sure!" Michelle left the stall and leaned against its half-closed door with her chin on the top edge. "Spout your big words. Do it right. Take all day. Take a *week.*"

. Stacey brushed harder. Maybe she was silly, but Mr. Lee was used to lots of fresh air, and he had to stay inside almost all the time until Breeze was stronger. Breeze wasn't going to lose him, too, not if she could help it. He was such a cunning foal, butting at them with his little black nose, grabbing at his bottle, grunting with delight. It was awful that Stormy had died—but having Breeze was fun.

"Stace! I want to go *now*! This minute!" Michelle gave the top board an emphatic jerk. Everything about her was emphatic: chunky body; round face; thick braids; brown eyes under level, dark brows which could draw into a scowling line when things went wrong. Her voice, even when it wasn't loud, somehow came at you. People always knew when Michelle was around. "I told you . . . the bus is *already* in the *lane*!" she exclaimed.

Stacey dug into a corner. "Can't you understand? I don't want to see it. Ever," she gritted between her teeth. How could Michelle be so excited? She herself was extra calm, only it wasn't really a *calm* kind of calm. More of a frozen feeling away down inside.

"We're missing *everything*," Michelle urged, teetering up and down on her toes.

"That's just fine," Stacey replied, as another thump joggled the partition between the stalls. "I'm not going. I still have to give Whisper her workout, and she wants her apple. You can tell me about it tonight."

"Oh . . . all right. But it would be more fun together." Michelle raced away.

After one last vigorous sweep, Stacey hung up the brush and brought in an armload of hay. "You can have a nice snack now," she told Mr. Lee, as she dumped it into the manger and then gave him and Breeze each a final pat.

In the next stall, Whisper minced toward her with a toss of her head. "Here's your apple," Stacey said, holding it on the flat of her hand. "You had a pretty long wait. Jealous, maybe? No need for that. . . . Breeze will never take your place."

My beautiful Whisper Please, she thought, as the velvety lips brushed her palm. It was three years since the exciting day when her father had bought the young mare from Katie McNeill, who had to move to the city of Portland. Ever since then, Whisper had been Stacey's

6

own, to ride and care for. She was a big horse of palest gray, almost white, hindquarters dappled with circles that scarcely showed except in good light, like the silver ripples on a lake, or wind-tracks in snow—the loveliest color a horse could be. As Stacey rubbed down the satiny coat and put on saddle and bridle, she talked softly, and Whisper waggled her ears. "You understand. I know you do," Stacey murmured, and planted a kiss on the long nose. "Bye, Brandy," she added to the dog, who was sitting up and thumping his tail on the floor. Although he could get in and out by his own low, swinging door, Brandy never strayed far from the barn.

As Stacey led Whisper into the sunshine, she asked herself why she had been so nasty to Mish. They used to do everything together, and people knew they were sisters right away, because they looked so much alike: dark eyes and thick, dark eyebrows; long, dark braids; solid, squarish faces with little dents in their chins.

And then, a few months ago, she—Stacey—had her hair cut short and grew out of her jeans, and all of a sudden years and years seemed to open up between them, with Michelle a pest most of the time. But that was no reason to act like a toad! She'd say she was sorry, first chance she had, to which Mish would grin and tell her "Aw, never mind." Nothing bothered Michelle for long, not even the horrible plan their dad had sprung on them, almost a year ago.

She'd never forget that time last summer—even

when she was old and bent and wrinkled and lost her teeth, she'd still remember every second. In her mind now she called it the Last Good Day. The day they found out what was going to happen.

It had started out as a wonderful, breezy, blue-sky morning, with clouds like white cotton, a Saturday when everyone—both parents and all four kids—decided to do something special.

Dad had elected to go fishing with Jeff, who was home from college for the summer.

Michelle had filled a can with worms from her precious worm farm and tagged at their heels, chattering without a break.

Linda, who wanted to be an actress and had an important role in the Rollins Pioneer Pageant, had stayed home to memorize her lines.

Stacey had been torn at first between spending the morning out-of-doors or curling up with a copy of *Jane Eyre*, in which she'd reached the exciting part about the mad woman. But the out-of-doors won, so she went into the canyons with their mother, whom they called Mar, to look for petroglyphs.

These—glyphs for short—could often be found in the dry, rocky land south of the Columbia River. Sticklike pictures of people and animals, of water devils, of the sun, they had been chipped into the rocks by long-forgotten Indian tribes. Many had recently been blasted off to be put into museums, or were covered by high water when the great dam was built. Many had been photographed, or copied, or published in books.

But others remained, hidden by brush in remote small canyons, and Mar belonged to a group of women who called themselves the Cliffhangers and were trying to make copies of them all. It was fun, Stacey thought, to trudge along a brushy ravine and investigate every likely spot.

That morning she and Mar had piled into the Jeep, along with a small mountain of gear, and clattered across rough, dry Lava Bend, named because it lay within the big bend of Cat Creek. Leaving the Jeep at the lip of a canyon, they scrambled to the bottom and spent the next hour pulling aside brush and staring at rocks.

"There!" Mar found the first faint carvings of antelope, just above a ledge. "Want to be photographer?" She handed over her camera.

After climbing to the ledge, Stacey took the picture, then handed back the camera and taped a sheet of paper over the design. "It makes me shiver all over," she said, as she chose a blue chalk from the bag at her belt. "Just imagine, Mar, people—real people—stood right here. I wonder what they were thinking about and how they felt."

Mar had taped a paper over another design. "Maybe not too different from the way we feel now. Loving this place," she said. Weekdays, Mar worked in town at the telephone office, where everybody said she was a tiger at keeping them on their toes. But today, in jeans and blue plaid shirt, she was friendly and calm, with sleek dark hair and slender waist.

Stacey began to brush with the blue chalk, which came off on only the raised places, leaving the pattern in white. "Anyway, somebody wanted this picture so much he was willing to work on it for hours, chipping and chipping with another stone."

It was dusk when the family gathered around the kitchen table for thick slabs of apple pie, made by Linda while she was practicing her lines. At first everybody was silly, trading jokes about the big fish that got away and the petroglyph that was out of reach, while Stacey held their little white house-dog, Suds, in her lap, and slipped him an occasional crumb. Although afterward she remembered that Dad and Mar had little to say, she didn't notice anything wrong until her father finished his second piece of pie and shoved his chair back from the table.

"Jeff . . . Linda . . . Stacey . . . Michelle," he said, naming them in order of age. He was the stocky type—not very tall, sandy hair, blue eyes, soft voiced—but when he spoke, they all sat up straight and listened. "We've been mulling over an idea, your mother and I." He gave half a smile to Mar, who smiled back. Sort of the same smile as when one of the kids had to have a splinter taken out and she was about to say hold-still-it-won't-hurt-very-much.

"We've made a decision, and we need your help," he continued.

"Sure, Dad. Anything . . . *anything* at *all,*" Linda promptly replied. Sixteen, with long, straight blond hair and blue eyes, she used to be chubby until she went on a diet because, she said, an actress couldn't afford to be gross. She was putting on an act now, Stacey thought— batting her eyes—lifting her chin. The Helpful One, or maybe Dutiful Daughter. Stacey wrinkled her nose at Jeff, who responded with a wink.

Their father cleared his throat again. "You know, of course, that wheat and beef prices are away down, and expenses up." He gave them another half-hearted smile. "Anyhow, you ought to know. I've complained about it enough."

"We understand," Linda murmured, poking out her lips in a way that Stacey knew was meant to be Full of Meaning. "We'll help you, Dad."

"You may not feel so helpful when you find out what it is," he warned her. "It's going to change . . . well . . . a lot of things."

"Are we *moving?*" exclaimed Michelle, with her mouth full of pie. "Crumb-bum! That really will be a change!"

Stacey leaned forward. "Michelle! Let him *explain!*" But she sank back again when Mar shook her head. "Trouble?" she whispered to Jeff, who nodded and pulled down the corners of his mouth. He knew, she thought. They'd already told Jeff.

Their father drew a long breath. They had to have more money, he said, especially now, with so many years of college to pay for, plus the new combine, which had set them back thousands of dollars. A wheat ranch was big business—and business was tough.

"I'll get a job," Linda eagerly suggested, but Mar said no—an education was more important. And that was when Dad dropped his bomb.

"We've received an offer that will give us a real boost, so we've decided to accept," he said. "We're going to lease part of the Rocking C." He paused, looking from one to another. "For a children's camp."

"A *camp*!" Stacey, who had been scratching Suds behind his ear, rubbed so hard he jerked away.

Their ranch, the Rocking C, was a large one, more than fifteen thousand acres, part of it in wheat fields, the rest stony and rough. They had cattle on that, and horses, which they raised for themselves and for sale.

Stacey thought the ranch was super-special, because one corner held the highest hills in the whole area, and she knew every gully and trail: where the tiny lakes shone blue in the sun; where streams were cool on a hot day; where to look for fossils or arrowheads. She had ridden Whisper into its high meadows, found a den of fox kits, slept under the stars. In summer she swam every day in

Fox Lake, right down at the bottom of their knoll, within sight of the house. All of it was hers.

"The springs?" Linda forgot to bat her eyes.

These were hot springs, the most special place of all. Really hot, too hot to hold your hand in the water, they welled up out of the ground and ran down to a cove of Fox Lake, making it wonderfully warm.

"The springs, of course," their father replied in a heavy voice. "That's one of the main reasons they want it—springs like these are rare, and warm water for swimming is a big asset. It's going to be an expensive camp, so they have to offer something special."

"They want Fox Lake? *Our lake?*" This was Michelle, who spent hours fishing from her boat.

"Part of it," he admitted.

"Boys or girls?" Stacey's insides were churning so she could hardly form the words.

"Both. Ages eight to twelve, with the usual activities. Hiking. Boating. Nature study. Maybe you can help with that, Stace."

Stacey drew a quick breath. Share her wonderful hideouts with a whole campful of strangers? City kids, who would strew peanut-butter sandwiches and paper bags all over Ox-Eye Meadow and trample the wildflowers on High Tor?

"I suppose they'll want to ride," she said, feeling as if she would choke. "On *our horses*?"

"That's a big part of camp life. They'll bring ponies for the younger children, but we'll lease them some larger ones, and. . . ."

"Not Whisper! I won't have a bunch of dumb kids spoiling her good mouth!"

"None of the family horses. Only some range stock," her father instantly assured her.

Stacey's heart was pounding. "Just the same, I think it's a *dumb* idea."

"We'll have a lot of kids to ride with," Michelle pointed out.

"*You* will. For me—garbage!"

"Stacey. . . ." Her father gave her one of his level, this-is-it looks. "It's the best choice we have. These people are taking a long-term lease and will put up their own buildings, at no expense to us. All the ranchers around here are under pressure. Some are selling. Your mother and I have considered every angle. And . . . it has to be done."

"All right. But I don't want to even *see* it." Stacey folded her napkin with extreme care and left it precisely in place. With a snap of her fingers, she called Suds to follow, then stumped up the stairs, flopped into the big, shabby chair beside her window, and gazed morosely at the hills. They lay against the evening sky, tier upon tier of deepening blue, with rims of snow on the highest ones. Campers! Right there on Fox Lake! They'd spoil everything.

After that, the Last Good Day, things never again were quite the same. When fall came, workmen started the buildings. All winter, while snow lay deep on the ground, they hammered and sawed the interiors. They built a dining hall, crafts hall, dormitories, boathouse.

In March, Linda was overjoyed to receive a job as part-time assistant in the riding classes, and Jeff reluctantly agreed to take charge of the camp stable. Stacey was asked to help out by guiding trail rides, not as leader —she was too young—but simply to show the way.

"Never! I don't want to even *look* at the camp!" she exclaimed.

"You'll like it better if you have a part in it," Mar told her. She was always urging Stacey to join 4-H or Scouts or take ballet lessons, but Stacey almost always refused.

"Like it! *Nothing* could make me like it!" She had exploded so violently that her parents didn't insist.

March had blown its windy way into April; April had turned to May—to June.

And now the bus had come, bringing the first campers. Pests, every one of them, Stacey said to herself as she led Whisper out of the barn.

Outside, the sun was hot, but a breeze carried the tang of sagebrush and rustled the stiff branches of mesquite. Squinting against the glare, Stacey swung into the saddle and walked Whisper up the path to the knoll where the rambling house stood, sheltered by its row of poplar trees. She stopped there, as she often did, to gaze at this view of the ranch, spread out below like a gigantic map.

Looking back, she could see the barn—white, a little shabby, with the other ranch buildings nearby, the corral just beyond, and Brook Meadow off to the side. This was the small pasture where they kept the family riding stock, because it was close and watered all year by Fox Creek. A row of gray-green willows straggled along the creek, and Tiny Lesska, their hired hand, was crouched beside the fence. Mending it, Stacey guessed. Tiny was always mending a fence.

Beyond the pasture she could see fields—some the tender green of new wheat, the rest black, plowed land that was lying fallow to gather moisture.

And when she turned in the saddle to look down the other slope, away from the barn, she could see Fox Lake, blue as a flower, with hazy mountains on the far side. Most of the ranch was bare of trees, but this end was a pine forest, not dense but open, like a park. No wonder those people wanted it for a camp, Stacey thought. Anybody would.

Although the camp buildings were almost hidden by the trees, she glimpsed roofs of bunkhouses, built of logs that she knew had been peeled and painted a slick, shiny brown. She curled her lips. Bunkhouses! They ought to see a real one! she thought. The longest roof—that was the dining hall and craft house—and the flash of white was the boathouse. It was just one big clutter. The lake shore used to be all wild and free, but now it was practically a city street.

And what was that? On the hill—a horseman, at the edge of the rocks. By his huge size and the way he sat hunched in the saddle she recognized him as Rod Wright, recently come back to run his family's Double Star Ranch, because his father had died.

The Double Star was next to their own ranch, and Stacey had seen Rod before, sitting like that on a hill above Fox Lake. She'd heard people say he was slippery, too friendly, too smooth, spoiled by his years in the city. She felt something closed in about him now, brooding and still. Was he planning? Scheming? At this Stacey almost laughed aloud, and told herself not to be silly, that she'd been reading too many creepy books. Of course Rod was curious about the camp, or maybe he thought it was a dumb idea, too.

Just then she saw the bus edge forward, and the next instant she heard a shout.

It had begun. The ranch was no longer their very own private place, but belonged, in a way, to a whole gang of kids. City kids, who wouldn't know how to take care of anything. And she mustn't even try to stop it, because Mar and Dad wanted the camp to succeed. *Needed* it, they said. No matter how she felt, she had to be nice— if possible.

But those kids couldn't ride Whisper! Or scare

Breeze! Or bother Mr. Lee. They couldn't even come near! She, Stacey, would sleep right there in the barn if she had to, every single night until the camp season was over.

2.
Victor Edward
McCauley the Third

Why did I do it? I'll never,
never as long as I live, be
able to figure it out.

—STACEY'S DIARY
JUNE 18

THE NEXT AFTERNOON Stacey led Whisper into the corral
and rolled some barrels into a cloverleaf pattern, while
Tiny, who had been moving bales of hay in the barn loft,
came outside and helped. He had been given his nickname ages ago as a joke, but he was tall and lean, with a
long, thin nose; long, mournful wrinkles beside his mouth;
long, bony arms and legs.

He lived alone in a little house a mile down the road,
and he drove back and forth every morning and evening,
doubled up in an undersized black car that sounded as if

every trip would be its last. Occasionally he took a meal with the family; more often he preferred his own mysterious concoctions, full of pumpkin seeds and herbs. Now and then he brought Stacey and Michelle a bag of dry, gritty cookies that tasted like hay.

Today, while Stacey gave Whisper a workout, he sagged over the top rail of the corral, big hands dangling. "Looks good," he said in a voice that sounded as if it came out of a well. "Your mare loves her work, and that's what it takes." Standing up straight, he pulled off his hat, exposing his high, shiny, bald forehead, and his voice dropped another notch.

> "Give me a spirit that on life's rough sea
> Loves t'have his sails filled with a lusty wind."

" 'Lusty wind!' That's beautiful!" Stacey always got goosebumps when Tiny recited, because his eyes turned misty and every word seemed to be pulled out of him from away down somewhere. Did he practice his poetry in the evening? she wondered, and pictured him in his dim little house, flinging his long arms up and down and really letting go.

But all she said was, "I'm hoping to speed up her turns."

"Good idea!" Tiny nodded his long face. "But mind you don't overdo it. Train her too hard, she'll get bored."

"I'll be careful." Stacey put Whisper over the course again, leaning toward the barrels, pulling her close, trying to nudge her forward at exactly the right instant. Although the day had been a prickly one, full of bitter thoughts about the camp, she felt better now. Talking with Tiny always soothed her, like putting lotion on a sunburn.

With the workout finished and Whisper made comfortable, she hurried inside, because it was her turn to cook dinner—meat loaf and baked potatoes, the things she knew best. Suds greeted her with an allover waggle, and she took time for one quick run through his tricks.

"Roll over!—Speak!—Dead dog!" She patted his woolly side. "Good for you. But I have work to do now." Pans rattled as she pulled them out of the cupboard.

Later on, when everybody had come home and gathered around the table, Michelle began to chatter. "They've got signs all over—brown ones with carved letters—ROCKING C CAMP." She heaped a slice of bread with blackberry jam. "There are a whole lot of kids my age. I *think* I'll get to ride with them. And they've got gym classes."

"We've leased the land," Mar said in her cool, assured voice. "We've no business intruding. You mustn't be a nuisance."

"And don't expect much!" exclaimed Linda, who had spent her first day on the job. "The kids couldn't wait to get on a horse, so we started a few at a time. What a mess!"

"I know." Michelle giggled. "I was watching."

Their father was grinning, too. "Pretty bad?"

"Well—I'm still alive. Barely." Linda rolled her eyes and groaned.

"I'll bet they don't even know how to hold the reins," said Stacey. "Sawing on the poor horses' mouths."

Linda drew a tremulous breath. "That's not all. Some are little demons. One thought he was the Lone Ranger and brought spurs. We didn't see them in time, and he got bucked off. Some are scared of a horse. One little girl threw up all over the saddle." Linda wasn't being the Dutiful Daughter, or Helpful One, or Noble Soul tonight: her face had a smudge, her blond hair was hanging in strings, and she'd broken a fingernail. She's real again, Stacey thought. My good old, friendly sis.

"And you, Jeff?" asked Dad, helping himself to another piece of meat loaf. "How did you fare?"

Jeff shook his head. "They're supposed to do their own tacking up, but boy! Is that wishful thinking! Most of them don't know a girth from a rein from a brow band."

With so much to talk about, dinner took a long time, and just as it was over, Stacey heard Brandy bark. He hears the camp and doesn't like it any better than I do, she thought, as she pushed back her chair. She'd hurry to the barn, so she could calm him down.

However, it was Linda's turn to clear the kitchen, and she looked so exhausted that Stacey offered to do it herself. By the time she had the dishwasher running, it was nearly dark, so she filled Breeze's bottle, snatched up an apple core and a carrot, ran down the path, and flung open the barn door. Brandy met her, growling low in his throat.

"Something bothering you?" she said, scratching behind his ears. "Well, let's have a look around and make sure everything is all right." With Brandy at her heels, she turned on the lights and checked the stalls. "Nothing's wrong," she cheerfully told him. "You've just been hearing the little monsters down at the lake."

Slipping into Breeze's stall, she fed Mr. Lee the carrot, while the foal bunted her and nickered. "Hungry?" she asked, as she held out the bottle, and instantly added, "Of course! You're starved." She smiled and held on tight, for he was smacking his lips and nearly tugging it away. "What manners! Hasn't Mr. Lee taught you better than that?" she asked, and when she heard impatient thumps from the next stall, she raised her voice. "Coming, Beautiful! Right away! I won't forget."

With the milk gone, Breeze gave the nipple one last pull, released it with a jerk, then arched his back in a string of baby-style bucks. "Frisky, are you?" said Stacey. "Well, it's time now for a nice, long sleep." With a final pat for Mr. Lee, and another for Breeze, she left them alone.

Whisper was watching over the closed bottom half

of the stall door. "Pretty Girl, how are you?" Stacey asked, slipping in beside her. "Here's your treat." She unwrapped the apple core, a fat one, because she'd purposely left it that way, and laid it on the flat of her hand.

The apple was gone and Stacey was quietly stroking Whisper's neck when she heard an unfamiliar sound, different from the horses' usual rustles and thumps. A sneeze? From the hayloft? Brandy had evidently heard it, too, for he was growling again and his neck hairs were bristling. "S-sh!" she cautioned. "Quiet, now."

After a long silence the sound came again, followed by a slight scrape and thud. "So—somebody's up there," she murmured, and Brandy twitched an ear. "One of the little brats from camp, I'll bet. We'll give them a surprise." In a voice loud enough to carry to the loft, she added, "Bye-bye for now, Pretty Girl. I'll see you in the morning."

She tramped heavily down the aisle, switched off the light, opened the door with the loudest squeak she could, and then banged it shut. But instead of going through, she stayed inside, with her hand on Brandy's head. "S-s-sh!" she told him again.

The barn was fragrant with the smell of hay and horses, and except for the thump of heavy feet, the rustle of straw, and an occasional snuffle, everything was still. In the faint light Stacey could see the stall fronts; the aisle, with its scattering of pale straw; the window at the far end, where stars showed through. Nothing more. She stood so long that it seemed as if she had been there forever, leaning against the scratchy boards and breathing as lightly as she could. Maybe she hadn't heard anything after all. Maybe she'd imagined it.

But it came again—a muffled sound from above. Someone was moving overhead along the center of the ceiling, all the way to the hole where the ladder and hay chute went through. Stacey heard a swish, and footsteps began to come down rung by rung.

They reached the bottom. A dark blob against the lighter color of the floor moved down the aisle. It didn't look very large—or did it? Maybe she ought to take off. But Brandy was right there, quivering and tense, so she decided to stay by the door, turn on the light before the person-blob was too close, and then, if it looked dangerous, run like anything. That ought to be safe enough.

Now? No. Not yet.

Now? Yes. A flip of the switch. And there he was— a small, thin boy, wearing a jacket over striped pajamas, and blinking in the sudden light. As Brandy erupted in a frenzy of barks and leaps, the boy tried to dart past, but Stacey grabbed him by a bony little arm.

"Hey!" The arm almost jerked free. "He's going to *bite* me! Let me *go!*" The boy's voice was high and piping, and he cringed away from the frantic dog.

"Not until I've had a good look," she replied, tightening her grip. "Quiet, Brandy." She hadn't expected anyone so young, with such scared, enormous eyes behind oversized glasses, or such pallid, waxy skin. He glared at her from under a fringe of blond hair that straggled over his forehead.

"Lemme *go!*" He spat out the words and tried again to jerk loose.

"Let you *go!* I'm going to take you to camp where you belong." Stacey held him with both hands as he struggled like a little fish on a hook. "Down, Brandy," she said, and the dog drew back. "Now. . . ." She turned again toward the boy. "What are you doing in our barn?"

"Lemme *go,* I tell you. You haven't got the right to grab me like that."

"*Right!* You talk to me about *rights*! You've no right to be here. This is private property." All the day's torment was rising in Stacey. "This isn't part of the camp, and you kids are supposed to *stay out!*" She gave the arm a shake, but not very hard, because the child was so small and scared.

"I wanted to see the little one."

"The little what?" As the boy quieted down, Stacey noticed that his jacket was new, and his slippers looked like real leather. Rich kid, she thought with scorn. All of them are.

"The little guy. The one you feed with a bottle. They told us about him this afternoon." He sneezed and wiped his nose with his sleeve. "She said there's going to be another one pretty soon."

"Who told you?"

"I don't know—a big girl."

Linda? thought Stacey. Trying to be the Most Popular Teacher? But then, with a pang, she reminded herself how bedraggled Linda had looked at dinner. She'd had a tough time today, maybe so tough she was ready to say anything she could think of, sensible or not, to keep the kids in line.

"Is there?" the boy asked.

"Is there what?"

"Going to be another baby horse pretty soon?"

"That's right."

"Wow! Two of them." The boy tried to wiggle free.

"Hold still," Stacey said. "I'm hanging on tight, no matter how you jerk. Now, listen. You positively can *not* come here all by yourself. You'll scare the animals." And make yourself sick, she thought as the child sneezed again. He was so thin and pale, and his eyes were so big, almost drowned in tears? . . . "Have you caught cold?" she abruptly asked.

He shook his head. "Hay fever. I think. From up there." He cocked an elbow toward the loft. "I get it lots of times."

"Hay fever? Well . . . you deserve it for trespassing. Now, what's your name?"

He looked straight ahead.

"Your *name?*" she repeated, giving his arm another small shake, which made Brandy rumble in his throat. And then, as she saw how desperately the child was blinking back tears, she felt her anger ebbing away. "Look, I'm not going to hurt you. Just tell me who you are."

"Vic—Victor." It was almost too soft to hear.

"Victor what?"

Throwing back his shoulders and lifting his chin, he spoke out distinctly, with a little pause before each word. "Victor—Edward—McCauley—the Third."

"Neat name. The third. Same as your dad?"

A solemn nod. "My grandpa, too."

"Grandpas are nice," Stacey said, thinking of her own grandfather in Ohio. "Mine comes to see us every Christmas. Does yours live around here?"

A shake of the head. "He's dead."

"Oh! I'm . . . I'm really sorry, Victor." Don't go soft, she admonished herself. Remember, he's one of those spoiled-brat kids from camp.

The boy was still staring at the wall. "My mom—mom—" He swallowed hard and thrust out his chin, pouring out the rest all in a rush. "She might die, too."

Stacey felt as if she'd been struck. What did you say —what *could* you say—to this? "Victor . . . I'm sorry . . . so . . ." she stammered. "Is she—is she—sick?"

Victor shook his head. "She got hurt. In our new car. And so did my dad, but he's getting better."

"And you came to *camp?*"

Victor sneezed and again wiped his nose on his sleeve. "My dad is—is real busy. He has to go see my mom a lot. That's why he sent me. He said this would be a real good place. He said I'd like it fine."

"Do you?"

"It's all right." Victor stared at the floor.

Relaxing her grip, Stacey rubbed his hand with her own warm one. "You're cold," she said. "But Victor . . . I think your mother will be all well again when you go home."

"Maybe." That sad little voice.

"Anyway, we've got to take you back to bed. Now, how did you get out?"

"Through a window. I came down a tree."

Stacey looked at him with new respect—so little and scrawny, and yet he had the spunk to break out on a dark night, scratch his way down a tree without any light, and enter a big, dark barn—because he wanted to see an orphan colt! Some gutsy little guy! "Here. Breeze is down the aisle," she said. Still holding tightly to Victor's hand, she led him to the stall, opened the top half of the door, and let him peer in at the colt and Mr. Lee.

"Wow!" Victor exclaimed. "He sure is a skinny one."

"Colts always look that way, because their legs have to be long, so they can reach their mothers to eat. But they put on weight fast."

"I thought his mother was—was dead." Victor glanced toward the tall brown gelding, with his white face and hairy white feet.

Was that why he had been so determined to see Breeze? "That isn't his mother." Stacey was almost whispering. "Just a really old, old horse, too poky to do much work, but he's nice and gentle, so we leave him there to keep Breeze company. Sort of a horse baby-sitter."

Victor gave a small, giggle that broke off at once.

"Little colts get so lonesome if they're alone that they don't grow fat and strong," Stacey continued. "This fellow's name is Mr. Lee."

"Wow!" Victor looked up at the long, placid, white face. "Does he bite?"

At this Stacey broke into a shaky laugh. "Bite? Mr. Lee? Of course not. He's the kindest-hearted old gentleman horse you'll ever meet."

"Oh. Well . . . can I pet him? The little guy, I mean?"

"I suppose so." There go my resolutions, Stacey thought as she unlatched the door and led Victor inside, with Brandy at their heels.

She released the child's hand, and he almost smiled as the colt whiffled and nosed into his palm. "It tickles!" he said, but shrank back when Mr. Lee stretched out his neck.

"Let him smell your hand. He wants to be friends."

"Oh. . . ." Holding his arm straight out, Victor stood

stiffly with his eyes shut while the gelding snuffled and bobbed his head. "He's nice, too," he said a moment later, opening his eyes again and reaching timidly upward.

Stacey watched the child stroke Mr. Lee's shoulder and slide his fingers through the prickly fringe of mane. "He's nice, all right, but we've got to go now," she said a few minutes later. "Breeze needs his sleep. He's just a baby, you know."

"Okay. Thanks for showing me."

"And now I'm going to take you back to camp." Stacey grasped the boy's hand again. "It's dangerous, Victor, to be running around like this in the night. You might get lost, or hurt. Besides, isn't it against the rules?"

"I guess so. Will they bawl me out?"

"Probably."

"Well—do you have to hang onto me so tight?"

"Probably. But I won't squeeze so hard if you promise not to break away."

"I promise."

Turning off the lights, Stacey led the boy outside, while Brandy sat beside his swinging dog-door and watched them go.

Clumps of greasewood were black in the faint moonlight. The wind was so strong that they hunched their shoulders and walked fast, up the knoll and down the other side. As they neared the camp, Victor hung back. "Is it pretty bad, sneaking out?"

"Pretty bad."

"Will they think I'm—well—worse than I really am?" He sounded anxious.

"And how are you? Terrible? Or slightly bad? Or generally pretty good?"

"Well . . . slightly bad, I suppose. Or maybe pretty good. Most of the time."

Stacey stopped at the corner of the bunkhouse. I'm crazy! she told herself. I hate the camp, and everything about it, including the campers. Why risk getting into a whole tankful of hot water for a sneezy little kid? But she knew what she would do.

"I don't want to get you into trouble the very first thing," she whispered. "Do you think. . . . Victor, how about that tree? The one you came down. Can you climb back up?"

"Sure. If you give me a lift to the first branch. It'd be easy." He held his finger under his nose to ward off another sneeze.

"And if I let you sneak in, will you promise not to run off again? Not to come back to our barn?"

"Cross my heart."

"Okay. I must be out of my mind, but if you can find the right tree, I'll help you up. That will give you one more chance to get started on the right foot."

"Really? *Honest?* Well—well, thanks." Victor pressed ahead. "Here it is," he whispered, staring up at the windows of the boys' dormitory. "No . . . it's the next one. Right here. If you'll give me a little boost. . . ."

"Okay. Up you go." Stacey released his hand. "Good night, Victor. Mind now—you promised."

"I won't forget. Wow! I'd never do that." With a rustle and scratch the boy was into the tree, and in a moment Stacey heard the window screen squeak, and squeak again, and a little thump.

So, she thought, as she started back to the house. The campers are here only one day, and already I've helped that puny little shrimp, probably the very worst one of the whole lot, to break the rules. But—poor little guy—looking for the colt. The colt whose mother is dead.

Turning, she started up the hill.

3.
The Owner
of the Double Star

He may be our neighbor, but he's
Totally Revolting. *I wish I
never had to see him again.*
—STACEY'S DIARY
JUNE 21

"SO I GAVE HIM A BOOST, and he crawled through the window, and—well—I suppose I've compounded a felony, or something. But I don't care. I'd do it again." Stacey, who was sitting on one of the beds in the sunny room, leaned grumpily against the pile of pillows. "Honestly, Gwen, he's the scrawniest kid, with great big glasses and teary eyes and a runny nose. Like a—a damp little owl."

Gwen burst into giggles. Small and curvy, with short, dark hair and intensely blue eyes, she was sitting cross-legged on the other bed, with a plate of cookies beside her. "Stace! The way you tell things! I can just see you leaping at him!" Another giggle. "Clutching him in your iron grip. Scaring him half to death—and then turning into such a marshmallow you *boost him into the tree!* Hurrah for you!" She stuffed a chocolate-chip cookie into her mouth and handed over the plate.

It was the Monday following Victor's escapade, and Stacey had ridden Whisper to the Circle K Ranch to visit her best friend, Gwen Krueger. Michelle, who had come along on her gray pony Tommy Rot, was outside with Teri Krueger, climbing a cottonwood tree, while the older girls had given their horses a workout around the barrels and then hurried upstairs to listen to tapes.

Stacey's world seemed brighter already. Whisper had run well, and besides, it always gave her a lift to be here, with sunlight pouring in, and music all around. Especially when Gwen had a plate of fresh cookies. Life couldn't be a total loss when you were eating something that scrumptious.

Still, she didn't feel quite easy about Victor. "My dad will kill me, if he finds out," she said.

"Oh, sure." Gwen dismissed it with a grin and wave of her hand. "Parents have to uphold law and order. Only. . . ." She turned serious. "That poor little guy. Dumped into camp while his mother's dying. You did exactly right."

"Maybe. . . ." Stacey chose a cookie that had lots of

chocolate chips. "It was the only thing I could do, anyway, just as if something bigger than me had taken over. But I hope he doesn't tattle."

"He won't." Gwen sounded comfortably secure. "It'd be his neck, if he did. Victor . . . is that his name? Have you seen your little pal Victor again?"

"Not a sign. But then, I've been pretty busy." Stacey had spent that morning at home alone—well, almost alone. Michelle had been there, too, jabbering a mile a minute, adding coffee grounds to her worm farm, giving Suds a bath in the upstairs tub. "We're always busy in the summer. You know how that is. But this year, with Jeff and Linda both busy at the camp. . . ." Stacey sighed. "There's a lot of extra work."

Gwen shook her head. "It sounds perfectly *repulsive.* How about dinner? Do you have to do the cooking?"

"Only part. We're taking turns, and Linda drew tonight. She'll fix Snails Supreme or something."

Laughing, Gwen slid in another tape, and Stacey tapped her foot in rhythm, listening with half her mind while the other half scurried round and round, fretting about the camp. It was a thought that nibbled at her constantly, like a mosquito on a hot night, until she was sure she was covered with round, red welts, all over on the inside where she couldn't scratch. "The awful part," she said. "The really horrible, miserable worst of it, is that it's a *horse* camp, so the kids will be riding everywhere. They'll throw soda cans in the streams. Pick the flowers."

"Repulsive," said Gwen again.

"And no matter how terrible I feel, I have to try to be a good sport, because Mar and Dad have trouble enough without me making it worse."

"I know. I'd absolutely die if we had kids trashing our land." Gwen popped the last cookie into her mouth and brushed the crumbs from her shirt. "But, Stace, as long as you can still go to Wyoming with us. . . ." She looked up. "You can, can't you? Or will you have to stay home, on account of all that work?"

"Oh, sure. I can go. Mar and Dad say they'll manage somehow." Stacey was quiet for a moment, thinking about the trip, which had been planned months before, when she was invited to accompany Gwen's family on their annual stock-buying excursion to the Wyoming State Fair. They would live in the family camper for almost a week, and the girls could try Stacey's Whisper Please and Gwen's Sky High against some of the best barrel racers in the West.

"I can hardly wait," Stacey continued. "Sleeping in the trailer . . . midway . . . roller coaster. . . ." She could almost see it—the crowd, the horses, the battered, determined cowboys. "How many days till we go?"

"I don't know. Let's count." Gwen took a well-scribbled calendar out of a drawer. "Here's one week . . . two . . . two and a half to the pageant." She was mumbling. "Three weeks . . . four . . . five—seven, plus three days. . . . Fifty-two days to takeoff!"

Stacey sighed. "That's practically forever. Oh, well, all the more time to get Whisper and Sky ready." She sat back, listening to the tape and thinking about the long summer, when she would ride in the crowd scenes of the Pioneer Pageant—the one Linda would be in—and then go to Wyoming. With all that to look forward to, she guessed she could put up with the camp.

At the end of the tape she glanced at her watch. "Gwen! We've got to scram! You come to our place tomorrow, and we'll practice again."

"Okay."

"I'll work fast and be through by—oh—two o'clock. Maybe sooner." After stopping in the kitchen for a final reinforcement of cookies, Stacey hurried outside, called for Michelle, and in a few minutes they were in the saddle.

"Did you have a good time?" Stacey asked as they walked their horses down the shady ranch lane.

"Oh, sure. I always do. Teri wishes she was me." Teri was Gwen's younger sister.

"Why, for cripe's sake?"

"Because I'm going to take swimming lessons. Every day, at ten o'clock."

"Swimming lessons! At the camp?"

"Sure. And a gym class, too."

Stacey pulled Whisper to a halt. "Michelle Chambers! Mar and Dad will hit the *ceiling*!"

"Why? It isn't one bit dangerous. They've got that

part of the lake marked off with a great big red rope."

"Of course they have. But Mish—*how did you manage that?*"

"Well . . . I went down there this morning, that's all. And Myrna—she's the girl I'm mainly friends with. So far. Myrna was ready to go in the swimming hole, and she said maybe I could try it, too, if I wanted to, because it's really our lake. And I did. Want to, I mean. So she asked the teacher, and. . . ."

"Mish! She didn't!"

Michelle bobbed her head. "Yes, she did. And when Myrna told the teacher where I live, she said she guessed it would be all right, only we'd have to ask the director. So Myrna took me to the office, and Penny—you remember Penny. She's the main person there, and she has hair just that exact color, just like a brand-new penny. That's where she got her name, only it's a nickname. Her *real* name is Anne. Anyway, Penny said it was all right. So. . . ."

"Michelle!" Stacey tried to wither her sister with a glare, but—as she grimly reflected—Mish was hard to wither. "We're supposed to *leave the campers alone* except when we have business with them. You know that."

"I *did* leave them alone. Well—almost alone. It was *Myrna's* idea."

"You aren't even supposed to be there. Mar said so."

"You're not my boss!" Michelle was turning red— coming to a boil, the family called it. Breathing hard, she urged Tommy to a swift trot, but flung back over her shoulder, "Penny didn't care a bit! She said I could, right away. Myrna didn't even have to ask her twice. So there!" Her elbows, head, legs—braids—were flapping with indignation as she jounced along.

Ask her twice! Stacey thought. Mish would, if she needed to. Ten times. A hundred. She'd march right up to the director and, one way or another, she'd pull it off. What Michelle wanted, Michelle would arrange. Stacey pressed her heels against Whisper's sides and followed swiftly along.

Twenty minutes later, with the quarrel forgotten, the girls were trotting on the soft shoulder of the country road, when they saw a Jeep in the distance with a large man standing beside it, leaning on one elbow and gazing toward the hills. It was Rod Wright of the Double Star, the man who had been on the hill, watching the campers arrive.

Rod's Jeep was close to the crumbling stone wall that somebody had once built, more or less following the line between his ranch and the Rocking C. Was he going to fix the wall? Stacey wondered. Why would he bother?

The wall ran across Lava Bend, which was broken by a network of ravines and stony ridges, with slabs of bedrock lying exposed and lonely crags thrusting against the sky. Its soil was so thin, its slopes so steep, that for longer than Stacey could even guess, nobody had taken time to repair the wall. Instead, the owners of both ranches had been running a few cattle on the Bend, letting them wander back and forth and sorting them out in the fall. But now—what did Rod have in mind?

When the girls came close, he lumbered into the road and laid a massive hand on Whisper's bridle. "Hello, Stacey—Michelle." His smile showed a lot of very white teeth. "I thought I saw you going by, a while back. Had a little outing?"

"Yes," Stacey replied, surprised that a rancher had time to watch his neighbors. Actually, he didn't even look like a rancher. A huge man who rolled from side to side when he walked, he wore boots—but they were new. His shirt was the brightest of plaids; his jeans were crisp, dark-blue; his fawn-colored hat was beautifully shaped.

"To see the young Kruegers, maybe?" asked Rod, as he briskly patted Whisper's nose. "Special friends?"

"We go to school together." Stacey stroked Whisper's neck and murmured her name, because his hands were rough, and the mare was shifting from one leg to another and pulling at the bit. "It's all right, girl. Steady there," she added.

Mr. Wright continued to thump Whisper's nose. He was built, Jeff had once commented, like a basketball on legs; his hair hung over his brow in dark wisps; and his smooth, round face was red and shiny with sweat. "Mighty hot day," he said, pulling a handkerchief out of his pocket. "That's right . . . mighty hot." He settled his massive form as if he were taking root and would stay there forever.

"Yes, but it's nice. It's always hot in June," Stacey replied, as Whisper tossed her head and snuffled. "Easy, girl. I know you want your supper, and we'll get moving soon."

"Pleasant, yes. Good breeze." Stuffing away his handkerchief, Mr. Wright fished in another pocket and brought out a package of gum. "Have some?" he companionably asked, holding it toward her.

"No, thank you." Be polite. He's our neighbor, Stacey reminded herself. Why does he seem so yukky? Because he makes me think of warm lard?

"I see the camp has opened up," Mr. Wright continued, expertly unwrapping two sticks of gum and popping them into his mouth. "Did you get quite a few takers?"

"All there's room for—I think," Stacey replied. "Actually, we don't have anything to do with running the camp. We only lease the land."

"Hm-m-m. Best arrangement, no doubt of it." The handkerchief was out again, mopping the broad red forehead. "Pays you a good sum? I'd bet a lot on that."

Stacey surreptitiously dug her heels into Whisper's sides, trying to make her so restless that they'd have to go. "I suppose. But I don't really know much about it." Why all the questions? she thought. It was her father's business, and she wasn't going to explain a thing.

Michelle, however, was never known to abandon an interesting discussion. "They pay us a *whole lot*! Dad says it's a godsend, with Jeff in college and Linda almost ready to start. Especially with acting stars in Linda's eyes. Dad says. . . ."

"The lease money will come in handy," Stacey hastily interrupted. "Every little bit helps, you know." She jerked her head sidewise, trying to signal Michelle to— for cripe's sake—hush up, and the little girl shrugged, while Mr. Wright, moving unpleasantly close, began to talk again.

"You're right. Every little bit helps, and everybody has to do what they can. It's mighty hard to make ends meet, these days. But there's ways . . . there's ways . . . if you can figure them out."

Another wide smile, and again that thought of melting grease. Was it because he was so sweaty? Or because . . . what had Dad said once? That time he was talking with Mar, just after Rod came back? Something about trouble? About being just barely within the law? And when she, Stacey, had walked into the room, Mar had shaken her head, and Dad had quit in midsentence.

Mr. Wright took out his handkerchief again, patting his head with it gently, as if he loved it and wanted to take extra-good care of it. "You could make really big dough, if you worked it right. Kiddies' camp—that's only a beginning. Them for the summer. Hunters in the fall. You'd double—maybe triple—your take."

"Hunters!" Michelle shouted, at which Tommy Rot snorted and tossed his head. "You'd let in *strangers?* With *guns?*"

"Sure! There's plenty of folks that want a good place to hunt."

Michelle stood up stiff-legged in her stirrups. "The deer—some of them—are almost tame! We leave them a *salt lick!*" She turned red, her shoulders began to heave, and Stacey realized that she was working up to one of her furious explosions.

Mr. Wright, however, threw back his head and laughed. "Got your dander up, didn't I, little girl? Just the same, it's a good idea—and I wouldn't blame your daddy one bit if he tried it. I know how it is—I have to do what I can, too, to make ends meet. Especially now I'm on this ranch. I've got kiddies to feed."

"Mr. Wright, it's late, and we have to go," Stacey firmly said. "Come on, Mish. Whisper and Tommy have had a good rest . . . let's give them a canter." Get Mish away, she thought, before she loses her temper and says something terrible! Or before I do it myself! Gathering up the reins and laying them sidewise across Whisper's neck, she gave her a kick that swung her around Mr. Wright and started her off at a brisk trot, with Michelle clopping along behind. When Stacey glanced back, she saw him still standing in the road, mopping his forehead, his face covered by the wide-open grin.

"He's *awful!*" Michelle yelled between joggles. "Do you think he'll do it?"

"I think he's just teasing us," Stacey resolutely replied.

But she felt uneasy. Rod Wright had been too friendly, too pleased. Patting Whisper. Offering them gum. Showing his teeth in that icky grin. He reminded her of a cat, a great, big, fat cat, playing with a mouse.

4.
Rod Wright Again

I wonder what he's up to.
Mish says he stinks—and
she's right.
—STACEY'S DIARY
JUNE 24

"HOME LOOKS GOOD. I'm hot," said Stacey, as they reached the lane and passed under the high arch with its Rocking C design.

"But I had fun with Teri," Michelle replied. *"Everything* was fun . . . except that creepy Rod Wright."

Stacey wrinkled her nose. "He's a toad!"

They found Linda in the kitchen, swathed in an enormous white canvas apron that had CHIEF OF CHEFS in red letters across the front. She was beating the contents of a pottery bowl, her nose was daubed with flour, and something was simmering on the stove.

Michelle drew an ecstatic breath. "M-m-m. Yummy! What is it?"

"Chicken Dijonnaise—I think. It's skinned, so it's low-calorie," Linda replied. "Also gingered carrots. And orange-mashed potatoes. . . ."

"Orange potatoes! U-u-u-ulp!" Michelle pretended to throw up. *"Putrid!"*

"It's in my *Slender Gourmet Guide,*" Linda stiffly explained. "You know what we agreed. We can all cook *whatever we want to* when it's our turn. And this is what I want." She lifted her chin in what her sisters called her Great-Lady manner.

"Oh, well—it'll probably taste good. Remember the time I tackled chicken mousse?" Stacey asked. "After that, yours will look like Julia Child." It was going to be an interesting summer, she reflected, with a gourmet sister on a diet, and a short-order brother, and herself somewhere between.

As she expected, dinner was strange. They were all there, even Tiny, for one of his occasional family meals. Freshly scrubbed, he bent low over the table and ate with rapt attention, looking up occasionally to beam and nod his head.

Although Linda pushed her food around her plate, disdaining most of it, the rest were hungry. The carrots quickly disappeared along with the chicken, but the orange potatoes huddled on the plates in soggy, yellow heaps.

"Pf-f-fh!" exclaimed Michelle, pretending to gag. "Even worse than they look."

"Not your best, Sis," Jeff agreed.

Tiny, however, looked up from his empty plate.

"Man misses much who fears to take a chance.
A change is oft refreshment,"

he said in his melancholy, quote-the-classics voice. And then, more normally, holding out his hand. "Have you plenty?"

"Afraid so." Linda's face turned red, but she smiled and passed him the bowl. "Thanks, Tiny. You're my pal."

Later, when she brought on dessert, she gave Mar an appealing glance. "It's strawberry sorbet, and I thought I followed the recipe exactly. But look at it! Practically ice cubes!"

"The flavor is delicious," Mar assured her as she tried to dig her fork into the brittle mound. She frowned and shook her head at Michelle, who was surreptitiously giving Suds a taste.

Later on, when Linda had gone to rehearsal, Stacey helped Jeff scrape plates for the dishwasher. "Poor Linnie. She was really embarrassed," she said.

He flipped a sprinkle of water at her. "Maybe so. But she might have cleaned up her own mess. Look at it! Every pot in the house, and most of them are stuck fast. Dishpan hands!" He held his up in mock dismay.

"What'll my little camp babies think? I'm supposed to be a hard-bitten cowpoke."

Stacey laughed. With Jeff, even washing dishes was fun. Everything about summer was fun—or would be, if she could forget the camp!

But no matter how she tried to do that, it was right there all the time, pinching her like a pair of outgrown riding boots. Even when she put it resolutely out of her mind, something always happened to bring it back.

One day, while she was working on the lunge line with Buttermilk, a two-year-old gelding that was to be sold, Mish appeared, carrying a bucket of sawdust and whistling at the top of her lungs.

"You must feel good," Stacey called out, as she let Buttermilk slow down.

"Yep." Michelle tenderly smoothed the top of the sawdust. "Big sale."

"Sale? Of worms?" Stacey managed to keep her tone serious, although Michelle's nonexistent profits were a family joke.

"Yep. A real good one. To Fritz."

"Mish!" Stacey almost dropped the lunge line. "You —Mish—you *couldn't*! He and Penny are the camp *directors*! They don't have time to fuss around with *worms*!" With a click of her tongue, she set Buttermilk to trotting again, while she pivoted in the center. "We're not supposed to bother them. It's bad enough for you to take those swimming lessons. But badgering. . . ."

Michelle set down the bucket. "I didn't *badger* them, Miss Perfect. They were talking to the swimming teacher about the kids wanted to go lake fishing, and what would they use for bait. And *she* said, 'Well, just ask Michelle here.' She said I was her *highest authority.*"

"I'm sure you were really helpful."

"Well, they're always asking me something. Do you want me to act like a dummy and say I don't know?"

"Oh—do it your own way." Stacey gave the line a flip, and Buttermilk stepped up his pace.

"That's what I've been telling you. And they were really glad to find out that worms work better in our lake than anything, and I have plenty of worms. So I'm taking them some now, because the kids want to go fishing *today.*" Shoulders twitching, Michelle started to leave the corral.

"Mish, I'm sorry. Look—I'm almost through here. How about a ride? A really good one, like we used to take?"

In a flash, Michelle was smiling again. "To Plunder Gorge? Or Rainbow Falls? Or. . . ."

"Wherever you'd like."

"Can we deliver my worms? It's right on the way."

"*You* can," Stacey replied. The camp again! "As for me—I'll wait on the trail."

She cooled down Buttermilk, saddled Whisper, and soon she and Michelle had ridden up the knoll and down the other side, stopping just before the last slope into camp.

"Coming with me?" asked Michelle.

"What do you think?"

Michelle turned Tommy Rot toward her. "Do you have to be so *stubborn*? You might at least *try* to get acquainted. You might even have some fun. I've met Myrna and Susie and Elfrieda and Sara Lou, and—oh— a whole bunch of kids. I'm going to roast marshmallows with them tomorrow."

"You've every right to make friends. And I've just as much right not to." Stacey rammed her feet into the stirrups. "I don't want to hear any more about it. I'm not —repeat, *not*—going any farther. Don't bug me about it." She held Whisper steady while Michelle rode swiftly on, with her bucket precariously balanced on the saddle horn. Near the bottom of the trail, several children met her and Stacey saw them run along beside Tommy Rot, around the corner of the main building, and out of sight.

For a few minutes the camp seemed deserted, but then a scrawny little boy, wearing swim trunks and carrying a towel, wandered toward the lake. It was Victor, Stacey realized, and he was alone. Didn't he have any friends? But of course she didn't care! Nothing about the camp made a scrap of difference to her.

He was standing at the edge of the lake when Michelle reappeared, accompanied as before by a bevy of children. They followed her up the trail to Stacey and gathered around Whisper, patting her nose and stroking her shoulders.

"Is this Whisper Please?" asked one little girl, looking up with wide blue eyes. "Michelle told us about her."

"She says Whisper is just wonderful!" exclaimed another. "She says Whisper won a whole lot of ribbons."

"Is it *really* true, what she said? Are you *really* taking her to Wyoming?"

"That's right," Stacey replied with a reluctant smile. "To the fair." She hated the camp—of course she did—and she always would, but these were pretty nice little kids. Their hands patting Whisper were gentle, and their voices soft. Linda or Jeff or somebody must have taught them how to behave around a horse.

"Whisper's gonna win," a pudgy little boy volunteered. "Maybe a whole lot of ribbons."

"Well—even one would be nice," Stacey replied. "But we have to go now. We're going to have a trail ride, and it's time to get started."

"We go on trail rides sometimes," added a solemn little girl who had been nibbling the end of her long pigtail. "Trail rides are fun. Bye, Whisper . . . Michelle. Bye, Tommy."

Stacey and Michelle turned away, but as she left, Stacey glanced again toward the lake where Victor was still alone on the shore, picking up stones and tossing them into the lake. Doesn't anybody even play with him?

she thought. Or maybe he's the one that won't play. But of course it didn't matter. The camp wasn't any business of hers.

A few minutes later, Whisper Please and Tommy Rot were cantering side by side away from the lake. "Where to?" asked Stacey. "Rainbow Falls? Plunder Gorge? High Tor?"

Michelle drew a long breath. "*All* of them—I wish. But I guess—Plunder Gorge. We haven't been there for a long time."

"Good," said Stacey, and started Whisper toward Lava Bend.

They wove their way around junipers and shoulder-high clumps of sage, passing the large rocks called the Castle and the Hermit, with pink spider flowers and blue penstemon in bloom at their bases. A ground squirrel sat up on its haunches to scold them, and a magpie darted away, squawking.

When they came to Plunder Gorge, they descended its long slope into cooler air at the bottom and stopped beside the sluggish brown stream to let Tommy Rot and Whisper have a drink. Water bugs with round, flat feet were skating on the quiet pools, and a canyon wren on an overhanging branch sang its clear, descending notes.

As soon as the horses raised their dripping muzzles, the girls rode on again, sliding off now and then to pull the brush away from a likely-looking rock. As usual, Stacey's saddlebag held equipment for tracing petroglyphs, and she made a hasty copy of a small carved elk.

"It's too common a design to be worth much time," she said as she rolled it up. "I only want it for a record."

She swung back into the saddle. A marmot whistled from a rounded rock; a hawk—a black speck circling against the sky—screamed its harsh notes. Occasionally the girls passed the dark mouth of a cave, high on the rock walls. Stacey had heard that outlaws formerly stashed their loot—plunder—in these caves, and although most people said the stories about them were made up, she never visited the gorge without wishing they were true.

Sooner than seemed possible, it was time to climb the slope again and start for home. They were still on Lava Bend, not far from the tumbledown stone wall, when Stacey saw a figure—no, two figures—on horses. One, of unmistakable, bulging build, was Rod Wright, while the other seemed to be carrying some kind of long-legged equipment—fence posts, she thought at first, but soon realized it was a surveyor's tripod, slanting across his shoulder.

"Let's go 'round," she called to Michelle, who obediently swung out. But they were too late, for Mr. Wright waved at them and approached at a fast trot.

"I see our friend wants to meet us," Stacey called.

"Do we *have* to?"

" 'Fraid so, unless you want to turn and run. I think we might as well make the best of it."

"Crumb-bum! What a pain!"

In a few minutes Mr. Wright pulled up his horse in front of them and mopped his forehead. "Mighty hot," he commented, with his oily grin.

"It's always hot in June," Stacey curtly replied. What was he doing on the Bend with a surveyor? She tried to keep Whisper moving, but Rod stood solidly in the way.

Michelle was sitting very straight, with her chin set. "I *like* it hot." She pressed the words out between set teeth. "I wait all winter long for it to get really warm, so I can go swimming."

"Swimming—ah, yes. Enjoy the lake, don't you? Extra-fine water. Warm. That's what counts." The big rancher gave her another beaming smile. "Have some?" he asked, holding out a package of gum.

"No, thank you," Stacey crisply replied. "Mr. Wright—we really have to go. We take turns being the family cook, and today is my day, so. . . ."

"Cooking, is it? Well—I know you'll put together a mighty fine meal." The huge man popped two sticks of gum into his mouth. "Don't be alarmed, you youngsters, about all this." He waved his arm toward the other man, who was plodding toward them with the surveyor's gear. "Just making some routine measurements."

"Measurements? On the Bend?" asked Stacey. "What for?"

Rod Wright shrugged his huge shoulders. "Ah, well. You must know your daddy and I both run our stock here.

The wall's bad, so I use a bit of his grass—he uses a bit of mine. It all comes out even-steven between friends."

Stacey didn't answer. She knew that the Chambers and Wright families had been friends, long ago when the ranches were first established, and had been living peacefully side by side for all those years. But she wished her father had fixed the wall.

The big man mopped his forehead. "Your land—my land. No matter who it belongs to, sometimes we need reference points. Not to worry." He spread his mouth in another smile.

"I won't. I'm sure it's all right. And good-bye now," Stacey replied, edging away. "We have to hurry."

"Sure thing." Mr. Wright was still beaming at them when they went clopping down the road.

"Why does he seem so yukky?" asked Michelle, as soon as they were well away. "He—he—what's wrong with him? He *smiled.* He acted nice."

"Nice, yes. Nice like a rattlesnake. I can't think why he'd survey this line—if that's what he's doing—unless he's up to something."

"About hunters?"

"Maybe. Or worse."

"That's the worst thing there is." Michelle bounced both feet against Tommy's sides. "Let's have a race. All the way to that biggest rock. *Go* it, Tommy!"

"After them!" echoed Stacey, giving Whisper a sudden squeeze. A good run was exactly what she needed.

5.
Fritz Has an Idea and Stacey Says No

---

*Of course I won't. I don't
want anything to do with
that stupid camp.*
—STACEY'S DIARY
JUNE 30

STACEY LEANED FORWARD in the saddle and patted Whisper's glossy neck. "Good girl," she said. "A couple more runs, and you'll have a nice, big apple core. I saved it for you." It was early morning, bright and cool, and she was working the silvery mare around the barrels, while Jeff watched from the corral fence.

"Hey! Try it the other way!" he shouted.

Stacey trotted Whisper toward him. "What other way?"

"Take her left and go counter-clockwise first."

"What for?" She had always started to the right, taken the first barrel clockwise, then reversed for the other two.

"So she'll have that left turn just once, and then two in the direction she likes. Either one is legal, just so you make a cloverleaf."

Stacey whacked the reins against her knee. Of all the stupid—*stupid!* She knew Whisper hated that turn, but she'd never thought of changing it. "Do you think she can learn it over?"

Jeff vaulted down from the fence. "It's worth a try. Walk her through."

"Okay." She walked the new path.

"And now at a trot."

"Right." A faster attempt.

"And now, let her go!"

Gripping the reins, Stacey turned Whisper left, gave her a sharp kick—and the mare stood stiff-legged, tossing her head. "Hey, there! *Move!*" Stacey flicked her with the crop.

At this, Whisper gave one loud snort, twitched her ears, and then, as if she suddenly understood, raced to the barrel, leaned far to the side, circled in a scuffle of dust, ran to the second . . . another circle . . . to the third . . . and home.

"Jeff! That bumpy lurch wasn't half so bad!" Stacey was laughing with excitement. "I think it's going to work!"

She tried again, and the next day, after a couple of practice trials, Jeff timed her and found she'd shaved off almost half a second.

"You *beauty!* You're so *smart!* The best horse in the whole world!" Stacey exclaimed. "A million thanks, Jeff. This has really helped. I can't wait to try it in Wyoming!"

She walked Whisper until the mare was cool, gave her a good brushing, and turned her into the pasture where most of the family horses were peacefully grazing: Tommy Rot; stubborn little Shoebutton whom the girls had all ridden when they were small; Mar's Lady Jane, who was soon to foal; and all the rest.

Mr. Lee and Breeze were there, too. The first time Stacey turned them loose, the rest had come to look over the newcomer. With an incredible racket of neighs and snuffles, they had nosed at the colt, then tossed their heads and run to the end of the pasture and back, hoofs pounding, manes and tails streaming. The younger horses had sniffed at him again and turned for a second run, while the older ones trotted a little distance off and stood with ears pricked and nostrils wide. But now Breeze was part of the herd, running with them and trying to nibble at the grass.

Later that week he acquired a playmate. Stacey and Michelle rode to Rainbow Falls, and when they returned, Tiny was waiting, his face wreathed in smiles.

"Come! See what we've got!" he exclaimed, pushing his hat far back on his high, bald forehead. "Just go

quietly in and have a look." His voice turned deep, and
he pulled off his hat and held it solemnly across his chest:

"Little creature, formed of joy and mirth. . . ."

Lady Jane! thought Stacey. *It must have happened!*
While Tiny took their horses' reins, she and Michelle ran
into the barn and stopped at the door of the mare's stall.

She was standing by the far wall, and close to her side
was a tiny foal. Bright brown like Lady Jane herself, with
a diamond-shaped white star, white sox and a fuzzy brush
of mane and tail, she was still so new that her hair stood
up in damp swirls. When she took a shaky step, her legs
spraddled apart and she went down in a sprawl. But she
struggled back to her feet and nuzzled Lady Jane's belly
for dinner.

"You—you *love!*" Stacey quietly lifted the door
latch, and the girls tiptoed into the stall.

The barn was dim and still, fragrant with hay, and
quiet except for the filly's greedy smacks. "I won't hurt
your baby," Stacey promised the mare, who whickered
and arched her neck, gazing at them with alert, dark eyes.
"I won't even touch her, if you don't want me to."

Lady Jane whickered again and bobbed her head.

"She's just *perfect!*" Even Michelle's voice was
hushed today. "I wish we'd been here when she was
born."

"Careful!" breathed Stacey. "Don't jerk." Cau-
tiously the girls reached out, but Lady Jane gave their

hands a gentle bunt with her nose and took a step side-wise, partly hiding the foal. Flies were buzzing. Stacey heard a clump of hoofs as Tiny led Tommy Rot and Whisper to their stalls. *"In* with you," he said. *"Git* in there."

In a moment he joined them. "Isn't that a fine baby now!" he exclaimed. "Just like her mama."

"She almost fell," Stacey said with a worried glance at the filly's tiny white feet. "Is she all right?"

"You can bet your boots on that. Not an hour old yet, and look at her—knows what she's after, sure enough. Takes them a little time to get their sea legs, but that one'll manage." He stroked Lady Jane's nose, while she closed her eyes with a grunt of pleasure. "Nice work . . . nice work," he murmured, and then, half to himself,

"I wonder, bathed in joy complete,

How anyone so young could be so sweet."

Stacey felt a lump in her throat. Tiny was sweet, too, in his own way.

A few minutes later the girls reluctantly left the barn. "We'll have to think of a *real good name,"* Michelle said with a bounce, as they started up the knoll.

"One that goes with Lady Jane," Stacey suggested. "Lady Mine?"

"My Fair Lady?" Mish wrinkled her nose. "No—too fancy."

"Lady Bug?"

"Hey—I like that!" Michelle gave another bounce. "Lady Bug. *Perfect!*"

Up at the house, where Jeff was putting charcoal into the outdoor barbecue, Stacey offered to make a salad while he shaped the hamburgers. As they worked, she told him about the filly. "Do you like Lady Bug for a name?" she asked. "Mish—" But Michelle had disappeared.

Afterward, when everyone had finished dinner and admired the foal and the kitchen was cleared, the family gathered on the breezeway. Suds was asleep in his favorite chair, Mar and Dad and Jeff were sharing the newspaper, Linda had gone to rehearsal, and Michelle, who had come back in time to eat, was hunting worms on the lawn. Stacey had just filled a bottle for Breeze when Brandy began to bark.

"Someone's in the barn!" Mar laid her paper down.

"I'll check," Stacey offered. "I'm going to feed Breeze, anyway."

She grabbed a flashlight and ran down the path. Victor again? Campers? When Brandy greeted her with anxious whines, she patted his head and said, "Good boy! Do those noisy kids bother you, too?"

Breeze and his big companion had been brought in for the night. While she fed him, she was alert, listening, but heard only his enthusiastic smacks, and Brandy, pacing the aisle and growling under his breath. Was someone in the loft? As soon as the bottle was empty, Stacey tiptoed to the ladder and stealthily began to climb. Except for the faint brush of her own footsteps and the sound of the horses rustling their straw, it was quiet until —was that a sneeze?

She reached the top. She bounded off the ladder, shone her flashlight all around, and there, peeking from behind the bales of hay, was a pale, little face with dark-rimmed glasses.

"*What* are you doing?" Stacey demanded, turning the light fully on him.

"I haven't hurt anything. Honest."

"But Victor . . . you *promised!*"

"I know." He tried to stifle a hiccup. "Only—you have a new one. I wanted to see it."

Stacey glowered at him. "How did you know we had a new one?"

"She . . . well . . . everybody knows it."

Michelle! thought Stacey. Of course—she'd gone to the camp before dinner. That was the reason she'd disappeared.

Victor looked anxiously at her. "I won't come anymore. I"—hiccup—"I promise."

"You told me that before. What's your promise worth?" Stacey longed to shake him. "Aren't you old enough to keep your word? You're not going to see anything, because I'm marching you straight back where you belong."

Victor grabbed her hand. "Hey—can I climb in the window again?"

"Climb in! I guess *not*! I'll take you to the counselors so they can lock you up." Stacey was almost too angry to talk. "Come along now."

"Can't I even see the little ones? Not even the one with the baby-sitter?"

"They're asleep. Down the ladder! Quick, now!" Stacey descended first, waited at the bottom, then took Victor's hand and led him outside. "Stay, Brandy," she commanded.

A slender moon cast its pale light across the rustling mesquite and sage, an owl hooted, and the black shape of a coyote slid across the path. When they reached the top of the knoll, they could see the dark cup of Fox Lake in the valley below, with lights reflected in golden streaks across its upper arm.

Stacey had met the directors, Penny and Fritz Heffner, while they were planning the camp, but so far this summer she had avoided them. Now, however, she marched Victor boldly up to the boys' bunkhouse and pounded on the door.

It was flung open by Penny, a tall, thin young woman with a mass of coppery hair, drawn back and tied with a ribbon. "What—! Has something happened?" She looked from Victor to Stacey with calm, gray eyes.

"I found this kid in our barn," said Stacey, feeling as if those eyes would look straight through her. "He's not supposed to be there."

"In your *barn*!" Penny motioned them into the hall.

"Victor! Why aren't you in bed? And how did you get out?"

Victor thrust out his chin and gave her an unblinking stare. "I climbed through the window."

"Into a tree," Stacey added.

Penny drew her mouth into a thin line. "Well— Fritz has to hear about this. He's inside." She led them into the camp's common room, where her husband, a stocky young man with a luxuriant black beard, was hunched over a litter of colored feathers, bits of thread, and fish hooks. Tying flies, Stacey knew. She had a vague impression of wood walls, white curtains, a big chair close to a lamp. It looked really nice—like a home! she thought with surprise.

As soon as they appeared, Fritz jumped up and held out his hand, which engulfed Stacey's in a firm, warm grip, like a friendly paw. "Is something up?" A grin spread behind the black beard.

"It's up, all right," Penny replied. "Up in the loft of their barn. Stacey found him."

"Hm-m-m." The grin faded. "Tell me."

"It's—well. . . ." It suddenly occurred to Stacey that certain details of her story would be highly uncomfortable. "We had a—a visitor once before, and I did a really dumb thing." Stammering with embarrassment, she went over it all. "I suppose it's mostly my fault," she finished. "I should have brought him to you the first time. But he promised not to come again, and I felt . . . felt. . . ."

"Yes." Fritz turned toward Victor. "You hear that, fella? She caught you in her barn. Twice. You knew you shouldn't be there?"

Victor nodded and wiped his nose on his sleeve.

"Suppose you take him up to bed," Fritz suggested to Penny. "I'll have a chat with Stacey."

"Good idea. Come along, Victor," said Penny, and reached for the boy's hand.

When they were alone, Fritz pulled out a chair for Stacey and dropped into his own. "Let's sit down while I get this straight," he said. "Victor's sneaked out of his bunkhouse twice and trespassed in your barn. In the loft, which I suppose is full of hay. Right?"

"Right."

"And the other time—the first day of camp—you helped him climb back into his room—*via* a tree?"

Stacey felt her face turn hot. "I—well—yes. I know I wasn't very—well—I wasn't thinking very straight. But . . . well. . . ."

"You felt sorry for him," Fritz finished for her. "As all of us do. He's an appealing little bugger, and he has a problem." Frowning, he twirled a black-and-orange feather between his fingers. "But that doesn't mean we should pamper him. Pampering never helped anybody."

"I suppose not." Stacey felt sure this was one of Fritz's guiding principles. "I'm really sorry. I won't do it again."

Fritz shrugged. "I'm sure you won't. Actually, his

mother is making quite a good recovery, but the kid is still in a panic, because she very nearly did die. And his father hasn't given him much support—he was quite badly injured himself and frantic with worry. We'll have to show a little tolerance there." He heaved a big sigh and picked up another feather. "Anyway, the camp hasn't worked out very well for Victor. He's pretty good in gym, but not on a horse, and he hasn't made friends. The original loner."

"I gathered that."

Fritz smiled again, showing his white teeth. "And I think we've solved a little mystery. The other day, friend Victor was singing the praises of a 'big girl'—not Linda —to one of the counselors—and when I happened to overhear and asked who it was, he clamped those stubborn little jaws together and gazed at the lake. But now I think I know."

Stacey's face burned. Victor *liked* her! And she in her heart had been calling him a brat, plus lots of worse things. "Anyway, I'll keep a close watch on the foals," she managed, wishing she could think of a Jane Eyre sort of comment, graceful and poised.

"We'll watch, too. Don't worry. . . . He won't get out again." Fritz fell silent, staring so long at the feathers that Stacey decided he must want her to leave.

However, just as she opened her mouth to say goodbye, he began to talk again. "I understand that you're not . . . um-m-m . . . not exactly delighted to have us here."

Stacey was speechless.

"I can see how you feel," Fritz continued. "You're used to having the ranch all to yourself. And now a bunch of kids, riding horses all over, is. . . ."

"O-oh!" Stacey's face felt even hotter than before. *"Who told you that?* Or—you needn't explain. It was Mish, of course."

No answer.

"Wasn't it? The original blabbermouth."

Fritz folded his arms and leaned back in his chair. "Let's just say she's forthright, which is actually not too bad a trait. One always knows where one stands, with Michelle."

"I'll say one does," Stacey muttered between her teeth. She'd have a score to settle there.

"Anyway, what I'm trying to suggest is that we have projects which you might enjoy. Especially the crafts classes—the teacher is an expert, and her projects for the older campers are quite unusual. They're going to work with petroglyphs next. And there's an excellent swimming program." He chuckled. "I think your *forthright* sister told you about it, but you turned it down."

"Oh-h!" So Mish had spilled that, too.

"Anyway, keep it in mind." Fritz stood up. "The offer is open, any time you'd like to try. Our oldest campers are twelve, and you're . . . ?"

"Thirteen."

"Yes. So they're close to your age. It might be fun.

You could do us a favor, too, if you'd show us some trails."
He grinned again. "I understand you're the family expert."

"No." Had Mish broadcast *everything*? But it sounded so bare, just the one word alone, that Stacey hastily added, "I told you that last spring. It's impossible."

"I'm sorry." Fritz shrugged and made a wry face. "Well—it was just an idea. Keep it in mind."

Five minutes later Stacey was outside in the moonlight, trudging up the knoll to the house. She wouldn't take swimming lessons at that stupid camp or show them even one trail. She *wouldn't*. She wouldn't even tell Mar what Fritz had said, for fear Mar would talk and talk about how neat it would be. Only—she kicked a clod of dirt out of the way. Only a crafts class that worked with petroglyphs. . . . What would they do?

But there weren't any "only's" about it. She'd given her answer, and it was no, and that's what she wanted it to be. One other thing was sure—she'd keep an eye on the barn. Even if Victor didn't come again, lots of other kids were down there at the camp. Anything might happen.

6.
Rod's Plan

*I knew he was up to
something, but I never
thought of this.*
—STACEY'S DIARY
JULY 8

THE NEXT WEEK PASSED in a rush. Stacey worked the
young horses they were getting ready to sell, took care of
Breeze, and trained Whisper. She laundered her pageant
costume and Michelle's and hung them up, starched and
ruffled. Just before bed every night, she drew a red *X* on
a calendar where she was counting the time. Twelve days
were left until the pageant and forty to the Wyoming
trip. Thirty-eight. Thirty-seven.

Early one afternoon Gwen stormed up the back
steps and pounded on the kitchen door. "Look at it! Just

70

look!" She unfolded a long, pink dress. "I should have tried it on sooner, but I thought it was okay—and. . . ." She held it to her shoulders. "It fitted me fine last year, and now . . . ! I can't possibly ride in it."

"It's—well. . . ." Stacey measured it against Gwen's waist. "Let's put it on. Maybe we can let it down."

"You'll see." They went to Stacey's slant-ceilinged bedroom, where Gwen struggled into the dress. "It's tight, too." When she started to fasten the tiny pink buttons, one popped off.

Giggling, Stacey helped Gwen squirm out of the dress. "It makes you look like a stuffed turkey!" she agreed. "But there are plenty more in our attic. I don't think any Chambers ever threw anything away."

"That's why I came," Gwen confessed, pulling on her jeans. "I knew you had a lot."

"Tons. We'll go up right now."

As they started along the hall, Gwen sighed. "It must be neat, Stace, to have such scads of stuff that belonged to your very own family. Mine never saves anything. Throw it out! Burn it up! That's their motto. They even tore down the house and built a new one."

"It's fun, all right." said Stacey, trying not to sound smug. She realized that Gwen's house was newer and grander and all-of-a-piece—but she liked her own.

It had been built over many years—first the cramped, little, boxy unit that had been remodeled into the kitchen, with Stacey's room just above; next, a towering section stacked in layers like a cake: basement, main floor, upstairs, and attic. It was decorated like a cake, too, with wooden scallops and swags and pillars, and even some carved heads high up under the eaves. And last of all, a rambling family room, added by Mar and Dad, with its TV, fireplace, and shelves for everybody's hobbies. The house had grown, as if it were alive, Stacey thought. Every house ought to do that.

"We'll try Lucy's trunk first," she said, as she pushed open the door at the bottom of the narrow attic stairs. "I'm going to wear one of her dresses—they're the best."

"Lucy's?"

"My great-great—I think it's four 'greats'—grandmother." Stacey led the way up the stairs, sniffing her first breath of hot, romantic attic dust, and thinking about her grandfather's stories: that Lucy had come in a covered wagon all the way from Ohio to Oregon to marry young Charlie Chambers; that they were the original owners of the land and built the first little house; that Lucy was beautiful and gentle and painted lovely pictures. It was like looking back and back at a dimly-lighted stage, the kind that had a gauzy curtain in front to make it mysterious and vague. "It was sad," she continued. "Lucy was only nineteen when her baby was born—and she died, so Grandfather Charlie named the baby Lucius, after her."

The attic spread around them like a cave, its corners shadowy and dark, where the ceiling came down almost to the floor. Dust particles danced in a sunbeam beside a window at the end, and it had a haunting, closed-in smell of time and age, old books and leather.

At one side, away back in a corner, was a spindly baby carriage with an awning like an umbrella. "I wonder what baby this held," Stacey murmured, giving it a shake which set up a cloud of dust. "Lucy's? And look, Gwen —a really, truly high-wheeled bike." She laughed. "I tried to ride it once and fell right on top of Mish. She had black-and-blue spoke marks all over her leg."

Sitting on a nearby shelf, half-hidden by a shawl, were a square, black typewriter and a phonograph with a snaky horn. Another shelf held stacks of dusty, oversized magazines, and still another was crammed with black iron cookware.

"I'll bet some of this is worth a lot," Gwen suggested.

"Maybe," Stacey agreed. "But Mar and Dad wouldn't sell it. They say it ties us to our past. Now—we want Lucy's little humpbacked trunk—and here it is! With her initials: L.A.C." They dragged it to the bright spot by the window, and swung up the lid.

Inside was an upper shelf like a tray, on which lay a bundle of letters, some ledgers and small black notebooks, and a bunch of dried-up flowers. "See, Gwen? The card says: MEADOW DAISIES AND LUPINE. LUCY'S WEDDING BOU-QUET. I saw it before, and it almost made me cry."

Gwen, kneeling beside her, picked up a gray account book. " 'One length red flannel, 15 cents per yard: $1.50.'

Imagine, Stacey—fifteen cents a yard! And ten yards!"

"For nightshirts?" Stacey grinned because Gwen had a smear of dust across her nose. But her own was probably just as streaked, she reflected, and rubbed it with her wrist. "Now—the dresses are underneath." They lifted out the tray.

In the main section of the trunk lay neatly folded dresses, embroidered petticoats and pantalettes, a box of tiny bonnets, and a pair of high-topped shoes with buttons and curving heels. "This is a nice one," Stacey said, unfolding a long, lavender-checked gingham. "I almost chose it for myself."

"It's pretty, all right," Gwen agreed. "But they *all* are! I want to see some more." She unfolded another, while Stacey plopped down on the floor with the letters beside her.

They had been written by Lucy to Charlie, in black ink with heavy strokes and flourishes, and old as they were, the paper was still crisp. "Gwen, listen! They're so *flowery!*" Stacey exclaimed, and read aloud: " *'Shades of evening have closed o'er us and finds me employed in writing to you. I was so happy to peruse your letter. I wish you would write them half a mile long, or nearly so.' "*

She stopped. "She's absolutely plastered it with the dearest little drawings. See?" She held it up, but Gwen was more interested in gingham and lace.

In a few minutes, Stacey opened one of the small

black books and found it was a journal, illustrated as the letters were. Lucy had written about their young mare and made a picture of it pulling a carriage with a fringed top. She described a picnic and made a sketch of sagebrush and juniper, mountains and lakes and wildflowers. When they built their house, she drew it with a cottonwood tree beside the door and labeled it "our precious new home."

New! thought Stacey. It was the oldest part of all; her own room must be the very one where Lucy had slept.

"Finished?" she asked Gwen, as she reluctantly laid the journals back in the tray. "We've been up here for a long time."

Gwen sighed. "Yes—I guess so. I'll take this one." She held up a blue-flowered dress with matching sunbonnet.

"Better try it first."

"Okay." Gwen slipped it on, and when they decided it fitted well enough, they folded the rest and slid the trunk back into place under the eaves.

By Friday, the day before the pageant, everything was ready. Stacey and Michelle had polished their antique sidesaddles. Linda had practiced her lines until, she said, she could say them in her sleep. Even Tiny had trimmed his hair—what there was of it—and Stacey had found him in the tack room, sewing a button on his best black jacket. "Got to shine up for Linnie," he explained, and added in his coming-out-of-a-well voice:

"Let me be dress'd fine as I will,
Flies, worms, and flowers, exceed me still."

"That's *nice*, Tiny," Stacey said. "Linda will be *so pleased* that you're going."

In the evening, after Linda left for her final rehearsal, the rest gathered in the breezeway, where Mar and Dad and Jeff shared the newspaper, Michelle sprawled on the floor with the comics, and Stacey burrowed into a library book, *The Yearling,* with Suds in her lap. She was lost in the story when the doorbell rang and Suds jumped down with his treble growl.

"I'll go." Stacey laid down her book.

She found Rod Wright on the porch, mopping his broad forehead and smiling his widest. "Good evening to you, Stacey. Is your daddy at home?"

"We all are, except Linda," she answered, trying to smile back. She'd had a horrid feeling all week long that Rod was going to start something—and here he was. But she politely led him to the breezeway, where her father motioned him to a seat, and Mar asked if he'd like some iced tea.

"I'd be right grateful for that," Rod replied, as he stuffed his handkerchief into his pocket. "My car's air-conditioned, of course, but it's still mighty hot everywhere else."

Comfortably settled, with the iced tea in hand, he came straight to the point. "Chambers, I've been checking over a few things. And I think we're living in the middle of a mistake."

Stacey's father frowned. "A mistake? About what?"

"The property line." Rod took a gulp of tea. "I've been to the courthouse and read the deeds, and consulted my attorney, and had a surveyor on the land. And that old stone wall is in the wrong place. Whoever built it must not've had a survey."

Stacey caught her breath. So that was it! Did he think he could move the line?

Her father set down his tea. "You think the line's off? How far?"

"A good piece. Like sixteen hundred feet."

Stacey could almost feel everybody stiffen. That was a lot of land! Half a mile? Not quite. But surely more than a quarter. Five thousand divided by four—She gave it up, because her father was speaking again, and she didn't want to miss a word.

"That's a substantial piece of ground. What's your basis?"

"This here." Rod pulled a paper from his pocket. "A copy of the original deed to my Double Star. The line, as you can see easy enough, starts from this certain petroglyph. You'll be interested in that, seeing as you folks set such store on them carvings." He handed the paper to Stacey's father, who read it, frowning, while Stacey looked over his shoulder. *"The fighting birds with one broken wing, the antelope, two devil marks, and the sun, high overhead."* There was more, but she couldn't see the rest.

"What d'you think of it?" Rod asked, when it was handed back.

"It looks official," Stacey's father replied. "However, I don't recall the petroglyph."

"Maybe not—but I found it sure enough, in a canyon on Lava Bend, and I made a drawing of it right there on the spot. See?" He showed them a second paper, and Stacey realized against her will that it was indeed a sketch of petroglyphs. "Fighting birds—two of them, with one broken wing. Antelope. Devil marks—a pair." Rod pointed them out. "I got a book from the library that has all the info. And the sun. Just like the deed says. Our great-granddaddies picked a lulu."

The Chambers and Wright families, Stacey knew, had been close friends long ago, living side by side on ranches which none of them had ever sold. They had helped each other through hard times and sorrows, rejoiced together when things went well. Surely whoever built the wall knew where the line was! *How could her father be so calm!*

"Assuming that's so," he was saying, "what does it mean, in terms of our land?"

"This." Rod Wright was really smiling now—a smile

that Stacey thought was in danger of cracking his head right off, just above the neck. She wished it would. "We started from the picture, Alf Stenger and I, and he's a right good surveyor. You'll agree to that?"

"Alf is competent."

"We surveyed the line, just like on my deed, and it goes on your side of the hot springs. In other words"— he was almost smacking his lips—"by rights, the springs is mine, and most of Fox Lake, too."

"And—?" Dad's voice was the soft, slow tone that Stacey knew meant he was hanging onto his temper. "What do you propose to do?"

Rod Wright laughed. "Do? Take over my land, of course. All of it, including the camp. By the courts if I have to, though you're an honest man, and it likely won't come to that."

"I'm honest. Yes." Still that deliberate, fuzzy tone.

"It's mine, fair and square. Oh—I'll pay the camp for their improvements. Matter of fact, I'm glad they had it done—the buildings and road. I'll make compensation to you, too, for that time you dredged the arm of the lake and sanded the bank for a swimming hole. It'll all be useful to me, for what I plan to put in. Never cheated a man in my life, and I don't propose to start now. But a kids' camp is peanuts."

"You have other plans?"

"I sure do. Kiddies in the summer, but come fall, I'll

make a hunting camp out of it and get the Big Money Boys from all over—California. The East. Charge them all the traffic will bear. I'll clean up!" The smile again.

Stacey felt as if she would burst. "Hunting? For deer?"

"Why not? Deer. Elk. Birds. Might even be some mountain sheep up there in the rocks, if anybody knows where to find them. Folks'll pay a good deal for a shot at one of those. Get them a nice trophy to put on the wall."

"But . . . but. . . ." Michelle had jumped to her feet and was turning red. "That's a *terrible* idea!" she hollered.

"Michelle!" This was the Mar that people said was a tiger at the telephone company. "No more of that!"

"Oh—well—r-r-r-rph." Making a growly noise in her throat, Michelle dropped back onto the floor. She said something barely audible, but Stacey, sitting close to her, could hear. "He *stinks!*"

He does stink, too, she thought.

Smiling, Rod brought out a map on which the surveyor had marked the location of the petroglyph. "Lucky I found it," he said. "But soon as I checked the deed, I remembered seeing that broken wing when I was a kid. So I hunted it up. No problem."

Somehow everyone managed to keep calm while they passed around the map. "We'll look into it," Dad said, still in a velvety voice, when Mr. Wright stood up to leave.

But as soon as the door closed behind him, they all

began to talk at once. "Dad! Can he do it?" Michelle shrieked.

Their father was frowning. "I don't know. I'll have to check our deed—should have done that long ago. Since the land has never been sold, I don't suppose anybody ever had the title searched, but the original ought to be on file at the courthouse." He was speaking slowly, thinking aloud. "I do know that old deeds often use natural features as markers—monuments, they called them—so Rod may be correct there." He folded his arms and paced up and down. "We'll have our own survey made, of course, and if he brings suit, as he evidently intends to do, we'll fight it. Provided the land's really ours."

"Brings suit? Can he do that?" Stacey asked.

"Anybody can sue anybody. Winning is another thing. But even having a survey will be expensive, and going to court—well, that could cost. . . ."

"The Circle C has used that strip for a hundred years, maybe more," Jeff interposed. "Isn't there some kind of law that gives ownership when you've had long-time possession?"

"We'll look into that, too," their father replied. "But with the wall falling down, the Double Star has been using that strip, too, just as we have. That might make a difference."

Stacey was squirreling around in her mind, wrestling with this terrible new fear. "Dad! If it's true—if he gets it—will he own Fox Lake? Our mountains?" She had a lump in her throat that made it hard to talk. Would Mirror Lake not be theirs anymore? Or Triple Falls? "Can he *possibly* be right?"

Frowning, her father looked at her. "He may be. I've been told that in the city he had the reputation of being not quite outside the law, but a smart, tricky operator. I don't think he'd start anything unless he felt pretty sure he could make it stick."

"We've got to do *something!*" This was Michelle, shrill-voiced and puffing. "Put him in jail?"

"He hasn't won yet!" Mar said, a red spot in each cheek. "We needn't borrow trouble until we check it out. Thoroughly."

"Tomorrow?" asked Stacey. "First thing in the morning?"

"Not on Saturday," her father replied. "The courthouse is closed. But Monday morning, I'll head that way and see what I can find. Meanwhile, tomorrow is the pageant. Did you forget?"

Forget? thought Stacey. Yes, she actually had forgotten all about it! What was more, she didn't even care. What did a silly pageant matter, when Rod Wright was after the very best part of their land?

7.
The Flying Bird with the Broken Wing

I've got to do something about it.

—STACEY'S DIARY

JULY 11

THE NEXT DAY WAS A NIGHTMARE.

"Don't tell Linda. Let her enjoy the play in peace," Mar and Dad both insisted, so all the while Michelle and Stacey were grooming their horses, washing manes and tails, and giving their costumes a last-minute check, they forced themselves to make silly jokes. They were sure Linda would notice them laughing too much, even when things weren't funny, but she was lost in her own excitement.

"Butterflies! Have I got them!" she exclaimed at lunch, wrapping her arms across her stomach. "No, Mar —not a bite. Not even an orange."

Stacey, Michelle, and Jeff were all going to ride in the pageant, so they loaded their horses into the truck for the trip to town and drove to the rodeo grounds. Everything here was ready. Bleachers stood on three sides of the arena. A stage had been built in the center for the speaking part—the part Linda was in. And searchlights were pointing toward the hills, where most of the cast would ride as pioneers, ranchers, and Indians.

Because the pageant was presented every year, each group of riders was led by someone who knew the action well, so the rehearsal was short. All Stacey had to do was follow along, keep Whisper under control, and watch out for Michelle and Tommy Rot. It was easy—fun. Or it would have been fun if she could have forgotten Rod Wright.

"We'll beat him," she told Whisper, who waggled an ear. "We'll figure out a way." But how? she wondered. He'd been so sure.

Sooner than seemed possible the practice was over, and after feeding and brushing their horses, Stacey and Linda, Jeff and Michelle, along with Gwen and her little sister and several others, went to the home of Allison Trudeau, who was in Linda's high school class. And there in the backyard, helping set a table for a picnic, was Katie McNeill, Linda's former classmate, who had owned Whisper Please, until she moved away from Rollins.

"You came!" Stacey was overjoyed. Katie was one of her favorites, because she had trained Whisper and had taught Stacey herself to barrel race. "I didn't expect you!"

"Did you think I'd miss the pageant? Not a chance!" said Katie, laughing. "How's Whisper? Is she in it?"

"Of course! She's the handsomest one there." Stacey drew a deep breath. "It was one of the best days of my entire life when you sold her to my dad!"

Katie wrinkled her nose. "Not a very happy day for me, I'm afraid. At least, I didn't think so at the time. But it's worked out okay." She raised an arm with her fist clenched. "Look at it—muscle! I'm still in gymnastics."

"And utterly super," added Allison, as she set down a pitcher of milk. "She's got a whole lot of medals." She laughed as Katie turned red. "No use trying to be modest! I saw them last spring, all over your bedroom wall. Framed."

"Anyway, I'm having a great time." Katie gave Stacey a smile. "But I still miss Whisper. Here—I've brought her a special treat." She handed over an apple in a plastic bag.

They flopped down together on the grass. "I've been riding a whole lot," Stacey said. "And I'm going—Katie, you'll never guess—"

"I know already!" Katie exclaimed. "Allison told me about Wyoming. Stacey, that's super. Whisper will have her big chance—and you'll have yours, too. I think she'll win something really important."

"I think so, too," Stacey confessed. "But I'm trying not to hope too hard, so I won't be disappointed."

Just then Jeff brought them each a hot dog, which they wolfed down because they had to hurry back to the arena. "Bye, Katie. Come see us!" Stacey said, just before she left.

"Not this time." Katie's smile was rueful. "I have to go back first thing in the morning. Concert tomorrow—my chorus. But I'll be watching you."

By the time they returned to the rodeo grounds, the bleachers were beginning to fill and a fat, orange moon was rising in the eastern sky. With Gwen on one side of her and Michelle on the other, Stacey rode Whisper into place, then slid off and fed her Katie's apple. But even now she couldn't forget Rod.

"Why did he have to come back?" she murmured. "If he'd only stayed—wherever he was—none of this would have happened. Maybe we can drive him away again." But she had no idea of how to go about it.

Just as Whisper finished the apple and gave her a nudge with her long head, Stacey heard the first boom of fireworks, which announced the opening parade. "Here we go!" she exclaimed, and swung herself into the saddle.

When the parade had wound through the arena and out again, and the play began, Stacey rode to their station behind a hill. Here she was too far from the stage to hear the lines, but close enough to catch the ripples of applause.

"Hear them clap!" Gwen, who was beside her, exclaimed. "They really like it."

"Linnie must be good!" Michelle, on the other side, proudly agreed.

At their first cue, the girls trotted across a hill behind three covered wagons, which stopped long enough for their passengers to scramble out and present a brief square dance.

At the second cue, Stacey and Gwen rode again, this time at breakneck speed, yelling their loudest, leaning over their horses' necks, and followed by Indians. Michelle, being on little Tommy Rot, wasn't in this, but Jeff on Cherokee was one of the leaders. It was exciting.

And at their final cue, Stacey and Jeff, Gwen and Michelle, were all in the large group, some riding, some in old-time carriages, who gathered for a pioneer meeting. Then came a splendid twenty minutes of fireworks—and the pageant was over.

Stacey had enjoyed the evening, but while she was helping load the horses into the truck she began to think about Rod again—his greasy smile, his fat, white hands. She wondered what Linda would think about him and wished she could tell her tonight, so they could talk it over. But that was impossible, because the cast was going to a late party.

The next morning they were all at breakfast when Linda burst into the kitchen, cheeks pink and hair already brushed smooth. "Mar—Dad!" she exclaimed. "You'll never guess. *Mr. Perry* was there. He sat right in the front row and came to our party, too."

"Perry!" said their father. "That drama coach you used to think had made the Earth?" Although he smiled, it was his mouth only, not his eyes.

Linda didn't seem to notice. "Who else?" She twirled across the floor to her father's chair and planted a kiss on top of his head. "And, Dad, he's getting to be a *really big man* in drama. Besides his teaching, he has a newspaper column every week, and he's *famous*! If I'd known he was coming, I'd have been *paralyzed*!" She flopped into her chair and struck a pose, chin in her hands and eyelids fluttering. "He *liked* me, too. He said I'd grown *immeasurably,* and this was the best work I've ever done! He said he always knew I had something special, but this actually *surprised* him! Imagine!"

"That's great, Sis," said Stacey, while Jeff jumped to his feet. "Let me feed the celebrity! Pancakes? The griddle is hot."

"Oh, yes! I'd *love* them!" Linda closed her eyes and sighed. "But only two! Calories, you know!"

"You might fill up, for once," said Mar with a twinkle. "You've hardly eaten anything for a week."

They were joking as always, praising Linda, letting her enjoy it, and yet the talk was all wrong . . . stiff . . . with little pauses where pauses didn't belong. *Tell her, somebody,* Stacey said to herself.

It was Mar, finally, who plunged in. "Linda—" She sounded so serious that Linda stopped batting her eyes.

"We had some news last evening that you have to know about. It's—possibly—quite important."

"Good news? Bad?" Linda asked, picking up the syrup pitcher.

"It's—regrettable," their father said. "We may lose part of the ranch, and at best we're facing an expensive battle in court." He explained Rod's threat.

Linda let syrup pour and pour until Stacey reached over and set the pitcher straight. "That's *awful!* Can't you stop him?" She wasn't being an actress now.

Their father sighed. "Stop him? I'll try."

And I'll try too, Stacey promised herself, if I can figure out anything to do. Sick Mish on him? The idea made her grin. Michelle could make even a rattlesnake crawl into its hole.

Her father was talking again. "For starters, I'm going to look up the deed tomorrow, soon as the courthouse opens."

"Can I go, too? *Please?*" Stacey exclaimed.

"It's a dull job."

"I don't care. I want to do something! It'll be better than just waiting around."

"You're sure?"

Stacey nodded, and Michelle said, "Cripes! Yes!"

"All right—come along," he replied, and turned again toward Linda.

Stacey only half listened to her horrified questions

and his calm voice, answering. We'll look up that deed, she told herself, and then we'll find that everything is all right. It won't be like Rod said at *all*.

Early the next morning, she and Michelle climbed into the car with their father for the drive to Ritchie, the county seat. "You mustn't get your hopes up," he said, his mouth set in a grim line. "There's a chance Rod is wrong, but not a very good one."

"But there *is* a chance?" Stacey was determined to hang onto that hope as long as she possibly could.

"A chance. Yes. A forlorn one."

"I hate him!" burst out Michelle from the backseat. "He—he *stinks!*"

"Not the most original remark you ever made," her father dryly reminded her. "And not the first time I've heard it. But I'm afraid . . . yes . . . that I agree."

He chuckled and Stacey tried to smile, too. Dad was a doll, even when he was so worried he'd probably not slept a wink the night before, any more than she had. She'd spent hours and hours staring into the dark and looking at the clock, and she'd bet he had done the same.

They drove through the spread-out little town, its houses set far back in the middle of wide, green lawns, with cottonwoods and oak trees for shade. Instead of yesterday's clear blue, the sky was hazy at the edges, the air heavy and still. The leaves hung motionless, and a robin on a high branch was chirping in fretful, staccato notes.

"I see we're early enough," said her father as he stopped in front of the town cafe. "Courthouse won't be opened for another twenty minutes." He gave Stacey a wry grin. "It just goes to show that it pays to be up at the crack of dawn. How about some food?"

"Food?" she asked. "Even the thought makes me sick. I don't think I can eat any at all."

"Well, I can!" Michelle exclaimed.

"Atta girl! The bottomless stomach." Their father exchanged amused glances with Stacey as they entered the cafe, which was heavily shaded against the glare outside, and cool with hanging plants.

"Really, Dad, I can't swallow a single bite," Stacey protested when the waitress brought them menus. But her father insisted, and, to her surprise, the French toast tasted so wonderful that she cleaned her plate.

Half an hour later, feeling much better, she followed her father into the county courthouse. On the outside it was plain tan brick, but the inside was elaborate, its lobby walls half-covered with black and white marble, its woodwork of polished oak, and a golden dome above the center.

They climbed the sweeping curves of a broad staircase to the second floor and found a door labeled DEPARTMENT OF RECORDS. It creaked open, letting them into a bare room where a ceiling fan stirred the air, and three clerks were rattling typewriters.

"Morning, Ben . . . Celia . . . Stu." Stacey's father

seemed to know them all. "We'd like to look over some old records, the ones that date back to the original deed for my spread."

"Deed records?" asked the clerk he had called Ben. A youngish, bald man with a pencil tucked behind his ear, he shoved back his chair, scraping it on the concrete floor. "They're public, of course. No problem there. Matter of fact, you're the second one that's asked for old records lately."

Michelle poked Stacey. "Rod?" She moved her lips to silently form the word.

Stacey replied with a nod, and rolled her eyes.

Ben showed them into a long room whose walls were lined with shelves, narrow as slits, and divided into sections that held gray record books. These were so large that each one lay flat in its own cubicle, with rollers at the sides to slide it in and out.

"The deed books are all in chronological order, beginning here," Ben said. He nodded toward two microfilm machines on a nearby table. "They're all on micro, and that would save you a sight of lifting."

"Thanks, but no," Stacey's father replied. "We'd like the originals."

Ben shook his head. "Micro's less bother—but suit yourself. Know what year the deed was filed?"

"Eighteen sixty-three—I think."

"About the same as that other fellow wanted. Fat guy. Real friendly. Now"—Ben ran his finger along the edges of the shelves—"here it is . . . sixty-three, two volumes, with sixty-two just there, and sixty-four on the other side, in case you need them, too."

"Thank you very much. I'm sure we won't have any trouble," Stacey's father replied, as Ben gave them a brisk nod, took the pencil from behind his ear, and left them alone.

Pulling off his jacket and draping it over the back of a chair, Stacey's father took out the first volume and laid it on a table with the other one beside it. "You girls can check this," he said. "We'll have to examine every deed until we find the right one—they aren't indexed. But you needn't read the entire document . . . just the first few lines of each, enough to see whether it's ours." He told them what to look for, and they all fell to work.

Entry number one was written in heavy black handwriting, with elaborate swirls and flourishes, and instead of skimming it, Stacey puzzled over the page until she had read it all.

"Such fancy language!" she said in a moment.

"I guess!" Michelle exclaimed. "Couldn't they use just plain English?"

"Listen!" Stacey read aloud. *"I do hereby acknowledge by these presents that I have this day bargained, sold, remised, confirmed, and forever Quit claim unto the said Morris, to his heirs, executors, administrators, and assizes all my right, title, interest, estate claim, demand, and property whatsoever, both at law and in equity deed, as well as possession as an expectancy of, in and to, all that certain piece parcel and lot of land being my land claim, commencing at a stake 10 chains North from an old cabbin erected by H. Browning which stands in a swail near the North side of Stone River and about 15 miles from Rollins.* " She looked up. "I wonder whether the person who wrote all that knew what it meant."

"Sure." Her father turned a page. "He was trying to prevent anybody from ever making trouble."

"Prevent trouble? With a jumble like that?" Michelle giggled. " 'Chains?' What's a chain?"

"Measure of length," he replied. "Sixty-six feet long. Surveyors use it because metal won't shrink or stretch."

Again Stacey bent over the book. "See those fancy circles beside their signatures, all curls and spirals, with SEAL printed inside. Did they think those made the deeds more official?"

"Doing the best they could, in a land that was hardly more than a wilderness," her father replied. "If this area'd been more settled, they'd have had real seals."

Slowly the girls turned the stiff pages. They found that, using chains and links, the measurements always started from a landmark, such as a large rock or tree, or even a building.

"Link! Part of a chain?" Stacey guessed.

"Right," her father replied with a nod. "The chains were so uniform that a link was always the same."

They read on. A fly landed on Stacey's nose, but she

brushed it off without looking up. A stranger came in, and she scarcely noticed.

A few minutes later she exclaimed, "Dad! "Here's the Circle K! Gwen ought to see this! *From the iron pipe in the cliff by the ferry landing, straight south 102 chains 12 links, to a witness rock."* She stopped. "Is that a. . . ."

"Landmark. What they measure from. It stands as a 'witness.' "

"Oh. *To a witness rock beside 2 iron pipes.* I wonder whether Gwen could find all that, if she looked."

"Probably," her father replied. "Most of the old landmarks still exist."

Stacey turned back to the book. The only sounds were the hum of the ceiling fan, the crackle of a page, or the squeak of the door as a clerk walked in or out. Michelle leaned against her and ran a smudgy finger over some lines, until Stacey brushed it away. She studied the spidery writing so long that the letters began to blur. Maybe it was a wild goose chase! Maybe their deed wasn't there! Maybe Rod Wright had made the whole thing up!

At last, when Michelle was beginning to squirm and Stacey was almost ready to quit, their father exclaimed, "Aha!"

"Have you *found* it?"

"Right here, all complete." He turned the book sidewise so the girls could see it, too.

"On a line running due South through the area called

*Lava Bend within the big bend of Cat Creek, from the
carving of the fighting birds with the broken wing, with the
antelope, the two Devil Signs, and the Sun high overhead,
where there are two iron pipes. From these to a witness rock
194 chains 12 links to the black rock above Crooked Canyon.*" There were many sentences more.

"Gul-lp!" exclaimed Michelle. "It runs on practically forever."

"It's long, all right," their father agreed. "They were
trying to describe it so exactly that nobody could ever
make a mistake."

The deed was full of references to chains and links
and degrees of direction, and to the "meander line" of
Cat Creek. "Do you think there's really a carving like
that?" Stacey asked.

"I'm afraid so," her father replied in a tired voice.
"This sounds like Rod's copy, and he says he's found the
glyph, broken wing and all." He read part of the deed
again. "Meander line—that creek has changed its course
a dozen times in these past hundred years. No help
there."

"Do you think we have any chance?" Stacey felt
disappointed and angry and scared, all at once.

"It's early days yet, Stacey. Don't worry—we'll
check it out. And right now, we'll get photocopies of this
entry to keep." He went into the outer office, soon returning with Ben, who lugged the heavy book away.

As Stacey waited, she was aware of a confused, half-formed idea—something she'd heard . . . or seen . . . or dreamed about. "Dad, are you sure that's the right deed?" she asked.

"Positive. The ranch was called Rocking C right from the start, and the Chambers family has lived on it ever since. There's no other ranch of that name."

"So you think Rod is right?"

He looked grim. "Things don't look exactly promising, unless the map has something to offer. Ben is going to bring it in, along with our photocopies. Don't worry—I'll try everything that gives us half a chance."

Good for Dad! Stacey told herself. And maybe the map will help, or at least remind me of . . . whatever-it-is. When Ben brought the map, she stood behind her father's chair as the two men estimated the location of Rod's petroglyph and laid a ruler along a line due south.

"Maybe that's not the place," Stacey insisted.

"He had a map, and his surveyor had located the glyph on it. This is it," her father replied.

And it was all too clear—the line passed, not on the far side of Fox Lake, as they had always thought, but through the edge closer to their house. Most of the lake, the hot springs, the camp, were all on the other side. Her father ran his finger along it, then sighed and shook his head.

Afterward, when the deed book was restored to its cubicle and the maps taken away, the three climbed into the car. The town didn't look so bright now. Main Street lay ahead of them, deserted under a glaring sun. An awning hung faded and limp. A car honked.

"Are we done for?" demanded Mish.

"Not entirely," their father replied. "We'll get Rod Wright to show us that carving, and see if it's where he says."

"And then . . . ?"

"And then—if he persists, as I think he will, we'll hire our own surveyor and see whether his findings agree. I've already called up Bill Norris, and he's ready to start." He turned onto the road to the ranch.

Stacey stared out the window as they sped along. What was that thing she couldn't remember? She felt as if she had a little door in the back of her mind, a door that had slammed shut on something important. Was it in the deed? One of the other deeds?

Something was there, just out of reach, behind the locked door. If she could find the key. . . .

8.
A Telephone Call
for Linda

---

*As usual, I opened my mouth
and put my foot in it. I'm
not exactly sorry—just
stunned, that's all.*
—STACEY'S DIARY
JULY 13

"TROT! TROT NOW. FASTER!" Stacey gave the lunge line a flip and pivoted a half-turn, speeding up Buttermilk. She had to hurry, because her father was planning to see Rod Wright's glyph pretty soon, and she and Michelle were going along. "That's better. Perfect!" She turned again, as the young gelding kept up a steady pace, hoofs beating a rhythm. "Now—easy there. . . . Slow. . . . Good boy!" She reversed Buttermilk's direction, took him around the circle twice, and brought him to a halt.

"Nice work!" called Tiny. "You keep that up, by next fall he'll be worth a sight more." He was leaning over the top rail, long hands clasped. "Mebbe 'stead of selling him, you'll keep him for yourself."

Stacey laughed. "Never! Buttermilk is a love—but he isn't Whisper!"

Tiny stood up and stretched his bony arms high above his head. "Good blood lines. Good handling. You can't beat it." His voice deepened to its fruity tone:

"It is a wond'rous thing, how fleet
'Twas on those little golden feet.
With what a pretty skipping grace,
It oft would challenge me the race."

In his own voice again, he asked, "Like that?"

"It's beautiful, Tiny. I always like to hear you recite."

"Yes. Well, about this barrel racing, just remember to keep your horses in tip-top condition. Because"—his voice deepened again—"the race is to the swift."

Stacey stared. *The race is to the swift?* She'd heard that quotation lots of times, and it said—she was almost sure of it—that the race was *not* to the swift. Was *that* how Tiny always had the right line on the tip of his tongue? "Tiny!" she exclaimed. "Do you really remember all those poems? Or do you . . . ?"

Tiny grinned and ducked his head. "Well—you might say. . . ."

"You can tell me, Tiny. I think you're wonderful."

Turning red, Tiny rubbed his hands on his jeans. "Well—since you set such store by your books, and since you're the first one as ever cared enough to ask, I'll tell you true. Some I remember and some I misremember. Some aren't quite right, so I fix 'em up a little. Shorten their stirrups, as 'twas, or let them down to fit."

Stacey nodded. "That's really good, Tiny."

Tiny hesitated. "And—seeing it's you—I'll tell you more. Some come straight out of my head." He shoved his hat so far back that Stacey thought it would surely slide off. "Everybody has to have something special— and rhyming's mine. I write it down, evenings. Got a little green book to put it in. Seems like jiggety words are always in my head, begging me to let them out." A wash of crimson started at his neck and spread up, across his chin, across his cheeks, all the way to his hat. "But I don't care to have everybody in tarnation knowing about it."

So that was Tiny's secret—and hers, now. "Tiny, thank you for telling me. I won't breathe it to anybody."

"I know you won't. Always were a tight-mouthed one. I've known that ever since the day you fell off Mr. Lee and never let on I was the one said you could try him." He started toward the barn, while Stacey gathered up the lunge line. She was sad, yet proud, at the thought of Tiny writing his rhymes, all alone in that dark little house, and trusting her with his secret—because she was the first one who cared.

With Tiny out of sight, Stacey led Buttermilk to the pasture, where she had already taken the other horses. No longer the fragile newborn, Breeze was standing with his legs spraddled, trying to imitate Mr. Lee's expert crunching of grass. When he saw Stacey, he danced up to her, wiggling his brush of tail.

"Sorry, fella," she said, as she stroked his forehead. "No bottle this time. You'll have to wait." He snorted, waggled an ear, whirled, and kicked up his heels in a baby buck that made her laugh. She was still watching him when her father honked the truck's horn, and Michelle shouted at her to hurry up.

They drove into the rough country of the Bend, with its network of gullies, its brush and crags. Rod Wright's Jeep was waiting at the lip of a canyon, and Stacey's father stopped his truck behind it. "So now we'll see—what we see," he commented as he jumped down, while Stacey and Michelle tumbled out the other side.

"Good day to you," Rod said with his beaming smile, as he fell into step beside their father. "We'll walk a few hundred feet down this canyon and find the carving easy enough. I've got it all marked." Teeth flashing, he glanced back at the girls. "You think the kiddies are up to the hike?"

"I think they are," their father tersely said, while Michelle flared: "We can go *anywhere!*"

Stacey gave her a poke and whispered into her ear, "S-s-st! Dad said we have to keep still and let him do the talking."

"That *creep!* But don't worry. I'll shut up."

They started down single file, picking their way between outcroppings of rough, gray rock and twisted, head-high clumps of chaparral. Here, with the breeze cut off, the air lay over them like a blanket, and the sky was a frowning gray mass of clouds. Locusts buzzed. A piñon jay scolded.

By the time they reached the canyon floor, Stacey was so hot that her shirt was sticking to her back. Although the creek in this canyon was only a trickle of muddy brown, she and Michelle knelt beside it and splashed water on their faces.

"It's right ahead, maybe three—four hundred yards," Rod said, and they started on again.

Everything was still except the crunch of footsteps. As they moved along, the canyon walls loomed above them, dark gray, with smooth, slaty surfaces. Below one of the largest rocks Rod stopped and held back the branches of a willow, to let them pass. "You can see it's all there," he said, pointing upward. "I've already broken out some brush, so's I could get a good look."

Stacey stepped forward for a clear view of the petroglyph—and there it was, well above their heads, with a ledge below it where the carver might have stood. As clearly as if she had the deed in her hand, she recalled its words: . . . *the fighting birds with the broken wing, with the antelope, the two Devil Marks, and the Sun, high overhead.* She named each part and checked them on the rock. They were complete.

Her father gazed up at them for a long time.

"Well . . ." Rod finally said. "What do you say now, Chambers?"

"It's—imposing. Have you found the iron pipes?"

"No pipes," Rod easily replied. "But I've got Alf Stenger out right now with a metal detector." He pulled out his handkerchief and mopped his forehead. "I'm told that absence of pipes is no proof. Drive them into a rock, they weaken it, and it freezes—cracks—thaws—falls off. Pipes get lost." He was beaming at them. "No hard feelings, I hope? You understand I can't afford not to claim what's rightfully mine?"

Stacey's father looked straight at Rod. "Naturally. My wife and I also would never retain what isn't legally ours. But before making any commitments, we'll have our own surveyor give us his opinion."

The big man shrugged. "If you want to spend your money, that's your business, not mine. It'll cost you plenty."

"I understand that." The blue eyes held a glint of steel.

Stacey caught a deep, proud breath. "Dad's fighting mad," she whispered to Michelle.

Later, when they were in the truck again on the way

home, Stacey leaned forward from the back seat. "I was *so proud* of you, Dad. You really stood up to Rod. I'm sure everything will be all right."

He shifted to a lower gear. "I wish I could feel as confident. Actually, that glyph almost has to be the right one. Every figure the deed names is there."

"Lots of rocks have glyphs all over them, put on every which way."

"True. But a bird with a broken wing? I've only heard of one of those. And that peculiar combination. . . ."

"Well—no. I guess you're right." Stacey glanced at Michelle, who was scowling at the gray-green sagebrush beside the road. Her eyebrows were drawn into a line, and her hands were tightly clasped.

"Our next move is to prove the location of the glyph and check its line due south, in hopes Rod figured it wrong. And then. . . ." Their father guided the Jeep into a depression and out again. "And then—perhaps a court fight." He sighed. "Which may just about wipe us out."

They drove home silently through the muggy heat.

A storm had been building all week, and when Stacey woke up the next morning, she heard the rattle of rain on the window. Pulling on a heavy shirt and sweater, because her room was cold, she went downstairs and found Linda in the kitchen, dragging listlessly from table to stove.

"My little cowboys will be beasts in weather like

this," she said as she poured a bowl of cereal and topped it with skim milk. "It feels like an all-day downpour. They'll be shut up. Restless."

"Maybe they'll go outside anyway," Stacey suggested. "I ride in the rain, lots of times."

"So do I, but we're used to it." Linda hurried through breakfast, put on rain clothes and left, letting the door close with a bang.

All day Stacey kept Lady Jane and Mr. Lee and the foals in the barn, where it was warm and dry, and she skipped Whisper's workout, for fear of a slip in the muddy corral. "We have to save you for Wyoming," she said as she gave the silvery mane and tail an extra-good brushing. "It's only three and a half weeks now. Time's going so fast!"

Late in the afternoon, while Michelle was on the lawn, happily collecting the bounty of worms which had crawled out into the wet, Linda stamped into the house, flung off her rain gear, and ran her fingers through her dripping hair. Stacey had a steaming kettle ready and made them each a cup of cocoa. "Was it as bad as you expected?" she asked, while they sat at the round table in the kitchen, she with cookies and Linda with an apple.

Linda made a face. "Worse, if possible. But I lived."

"Tomorrow will be better." Stacey had a warm, cozy feeling as they sat there together, listening to rain on the windows, not talking much, but comfortable and close.

Just as she was pouring their second cups, the telephone rang, and a man's voice asked for Linda, explaining that he was in California. "Long distance, Linnie," said Stacey, handing it over. "A man, and he sounds awfully —awfully crisp."

"Crisp?" Linda whispered, wrinkling her nose. "I can't imagine who. . . ." She spoke into the receiver. "Hello . . . oh! *Hello!*" There was a long pause as the voice talked on and on. "Why—thank you." Her cheeks had turned pink, and her lips curved in a smile.

Another long pause. "In *LaRue?* When?" A briefer pause, and Linda's shoulders sagged. "I'm sorry, Mr. Perry. *Really* sorry. But it's impossible." She sounded as if she'd swallowed something the wrong way, and it made her choke. "No, not a chance." With a quick good-bye, she replaced the telephone and dashed out of the room, leaving her cocoa on the table.

Hm-m-m. Stacey nibbled another cookie. Mr. Perry. Linda's old teacher, who had come to the pageant, had evidently asked her to do something special. But she'd turned him down. Why? Stuffing the cookie into her mouth, Stacey pounded up the stairs.

She found her sister facedown on the bed, muffling sobs in a pillow, with Suds cuddled in the crook of her arm. "Linnie!" Stacey gasped. *"Tell* me!"

Linda pulled Suds closer.

"Linnie—Linnie," Stacey murmured, rubbing the back of her sister's neck. "You'll feel better if you talk about it." When there was still no answer, she raised her voice. *"Hey!* I always tell you things. Like when Mar and Dad decided to lease the camp. I really exploded."

Stacey sat silent, continuing to rub. "That feels good," Linda said at last, her voice muffled by the pillow. "Don't stop."

"Sure." Stacey tried to remember what she'd heard about LaRue. Of course! It was that old mining town in the California mountains, the one with the summer theater. Linda had applied for its student scholarship, but it had already been awarded. So. . . .

"Linnie—did Mr. Perry offer you a part in a play?"

Linda moved her head on the pillow in an abbreviated nod.

"And you *turned it down?* Why, for cripe's sake?"

Linda rolled over and propped herself on one elbow. "It's *awful.* He said the director at LaRue called him this afternoon because their scholarship student went skating and broke her ankle." Tears were streaming down her cheeks. "They need somebody in a hurry—and said they'd hire whoever Mr. Perry recommended."

"Well, that's really neat."

"But Stace—don't you see?—I've promised Penny and Fritz." Linda's voice had risen to a wail. "Penny told me they borrowed every cent they could to build the camp, so they don't have any to spare—and having a camp is their dream—and I can't just—walk out—on them." She was crying again.

"They could get somebody else," Stacey insisted.

"For the classes—sure. But I'm the trail guide, too. If I let them down, they can only take the kids to the same old places, over and over and over."

"Jeff?"

"He already leads a few. But they ought to have two guys at the stable, not just one. He can't take on anything extra. And Sunday is Parents' Day. My kids have *practiced* for it."

When Stacey handed her a tissue, Linda blew her nose, then continued more calmly. "It would really hurt the camp. You can see that."

"Well—sure. But cripe's sake, Penny and Fritz wouldn't expect you to turn down a chance like that."

"Maybe not. But I'm not going to put them on the spot by asking."

"You ought to talk to Mar and Dad."

Linda shook her head. "No." She grabbed Stacey by the arm. "And *don't you dare tell them.* They already have trouble enough."

"Of course I'll tell them! They'd want to know!"

"*No,* I tell you. It's *my* affair. Nobody else's." Linda stormed at her until Stacey promised.

But as she went back downstairs, she brooded. It wasn't fair for Linda to pass this up. If the camp really had to have her, maybe it was her duty—but surely there was another way.

Another way—yes! An awful one! *Why* had she thought of it? *Why* couldn't she ever leave well enough alone? But, like it or not, the idea was there and she'd never get rid of it now. It would leer at her, nag at her, haunt her forever unless she followed it through. *So—get it over!* she scolded herself.

Throwing on her plastic rain gear and grabbing one more cookie from the jar, she marched rapidly up the knoll and down the other side, lifting her face to the rain and setting her feet down with a splattery squelch. Maybe —if she was lucky—her Dazzling Project wouldn't work. Maybe Penny and Fritz would only laugh. But then— *what about Linda?*

She rounded the end of the lake and banged on the door of the main lodge, which Penny opened almost at once. "Stacey! Out in this?" she exclaimed. "Come in where it's warm." She led the way into the common room.

Fritz was there, bent over a large chart spread out on the table. "Hey!" he rumbled. "Did you walk or swim?"

"I like the rain," Stacey briefly replied as she shook the water off her jacket. "It'll make the range nice and green. But. . . ." She looked around. "No kids?"

Fritz grinned. "Even a proxy-parent needs a rest now and then. Actually, they're having their free hour before dinner, and we sent them all out—*out!*" He spread his arms in a Dracula-gesture. "Under guard of course. Swaddled in enough plastic to make a circus tent. While Pen and I plan a mystery game for this evening."

Stacey glanced at the chart, which was laid out like

rooms, with clues in each. "You have a victim?" she asked.

"Sure. The worst loudmouth in camp. It'll keep him quiet for once," Fritz replied with another grin. "But enough of that—something earthshaking must have brought you out in this downpour."

"Well . . . it's pretty important. Linda has an awful problem." As quickly as she could, Stacey told them about the telephone call, and Linda's decision. "I thought. . . ." She faltered before the serious expressions on both of their faces.

"Linda—Linda—well, she'd be hard to replace," Penny said slowly, choosing her words. "There's the gymkhana for Parents' Day so the kids can show what they've learned about riding. They'll need Linda for that. And she's planned a special overnight to High Tor, which we've already included in the new brochure. And Jeff. . . ."

"Pen, you're not thinking!" exploded Fritz. "Of course Linda is to take the job, and we'll manage. I'll go up and talk to her about it myself, right now."

"But the point . . ." Stacey objected. "The point is that she's made up her mind not to let you down. No matter how many times you tell her okay, go ahead, she won't do it. You'll have to think of a really good plan first. So. . . ." She gulped. Big-hearted Stacey! She'd better say it as fast as she could, before she changed her mind. "So *I'll do it for her!* I know the trails even better than she does. If you get a teacher for the classes, I mean. . . ."

What kind of trap am I getting myself into? she thought. *But it's done! I can't back down now!*

Penny pushed her coppery hair back from her forehead. "Fritz, I think we'd better take this up with Linda. I'll stay here to meet the campers when they come in, and you go up to the house." She motioned to him, and they moved toward a corner.

"Excuse us a minute, Stacey," Fritz said. "Conference time!"

While they talked together, Stacey stood at the window and gazed at the rain. The hikers were returning, far down on the path beside the lake. They were dressed in waterproof coats and hats—blue—red—yellow—wet and shiny, and she could faintly hear them singing interminable verses of "She'll Be Comin' Round the Mountain." They didn't look very big out there, trudging along. Just a bunch of wet little kids—and not much of a threat, compared to Rod Wright.

A few minutes later, she found herself outside again, slogging up the knoll with Fritz, while gobs of mud weighted her boots and rain dripped off the end of her nose. But the storm inside was even worse. So! Heroic Stacey! she scolded herself. What have you got in your head? Bran flakes? Offering to steer these dumb-dumb campers on their dumb-dumb hikes! *Don't you ever think?* Well, *think about it now!*

It was bad enough to get tangled up in that miserable

camp. But if Penny and Fritz took her up on her Big, Noble, Generous Offer—if they let her be the camp guide —she'd have to stay home to do it. That meant she couldn't go to Wyoming.

9.
The Day of the Gymkhana

*I don't see how a father could
do that. Poor little guy.*
—STACEY'S DIARY
JULY 17

WHEN STACEY AND FRITZ reached the house, Michelle
was trudging back and forth from kitchen to dining room,
slapping dishes onto the table, because it was Jeff's turn
to cook, and she'd offered to help. Jeff himself was in the
kitchen, patting out hamburgers—his standard menu.
"Have Mar and Dad come in?" Stacey asked. "And have
you seen Linda?"

Jeff looked up with a grin. "Nobody's here but me
and Mish. Lin's upstairs, I suppose—she left camp before
I did. But she's in seclusion."

"I'll find her," Stacey replied. "Fritz is here, Jeff. He
wants to see her."

"Hi! Can I help?" suggested Fritz, who had followed her in. "I wield a mean paring knife."

"Good. Try it out on these." Jeff waved toward a pan of potatoes. "For fries." As Stacey left, they were talking about the relative chances of the Dodgers and Giants in the Saturday game.

Upstairs, Stacey found Linda perched on the edge of the bed, carefully applying nail polish from a bottle that stood on the night stand. Although her eyes were red, her hair was brushed, and she was wearing fresh lipstick. "Sorry about that scene, sis," she said. "I've decided to call off the wake. And many thanks for the TLC."

"Anytime," Stacey replied, feeling awkward. "Linda, Fritz is downstairs to see you. He wants . . . ."

"Fritz? Why . . . ?" For a moment Linda looked puzzled; then she set her lips in a stubborn line. "I know what he wants, and it's no use. I've made up my mind." She wasn't acting now, just biting off her words, with her chin in the air.

"I really think he has a pretty good plan," Stacey said. "Can't you at least hear about it?"

"Stace!" Linda's eyes suddenly brimmed with tears. "Do you think this is easy for me? Now you just go right down and . . . . *Stace!*" It was a most inelegant yell. "How did he *know?* Unless you blabbed about poor little Linda!" She doubled her hands into fists, then jerked them apart. "Look at my nails! Smeared. I'll have to start all over! And it's *your fault!*"

"*My fault?*" Stacey exploded. "You haven't even let me tell you what Fritz wants. You haven't the *manners* to . . . ."

"*Manners!*" Linda shrieked. "What do *manners* have to do with it? You betrayed a *confidence*. Why didn't you keep your *big mouth shut?*" She jerked at the bottle of polish and spilled it on her jeans. "*Look* what you've made me do. Little Miss Nosy! Just *look!*"

"Blame it on me! Sure! When it's your own stupid . . . ."

At this moment the door opened, and Mar stood there, still in her dark blue office skirt and blouse. "Girls!" she exclaimed, not loudly, but in the way that meant Enough of That Nonsense. "I could hear you the moment I opened the front door! *What* is going on?"

"She ratted on me!" Linda muttered, at the same instant that Stacey jerked out, "She won't even *listen.*" But Mar merely closed the door and stood quietly leaning against it with her arms folded.

"Now, let's talk this over," she said, while the girls glared at one another. "You'll each have a chance, with no interruptions. Linda first."

"There's absolutely no need for discussion. It's my affair," Linda muttered, gazing at the wall.

"*And* mine!" This was Stacey.

Mar dropped into a chair. "*And* you obviously need a referee. So—Linda?"

The Day of the Gymkhana

Glowering, Linda dampened a bit of cotton and dabbed at her fingernails, savagely, as if she'd rub them off. Hesitantly at first, then more freely, she explained the telephone call and her decision. "I've already told Mr. Perry that I can't come," she said as she recapped a bottle. "It's settled—done—concluded. This little conference is a complete waste of time."

"We'll see about that. Now—Stacey?"

Forcing herself to speak calmly and slowly, although her breath was coming in jerks, Stacey described her offer to Fritz and Penny. "I can go to Wyoming next year, instead," she finished. "It's no—no big—" Could she say it, with that lump in her throat? "No big—deal." *Liar,* she fiercely told herself. *It's the biggest deal you've ever had.*

When she was through, Mar looked at her as if she'd never quite seen her before. "You'd pass up the fair?"

"Yes." Stacey stared at her own feet and decided she might as well tell a whopper as a half-baked fib. "I don't really care all that much. There are—lots of other places —to ride."

After sitting quietly for a moment, Mar opened the door. "I think we'd better talk this over with Fritz and your father, if he's here in time. Come along now."

Our tiger-mom. She can purr, but she can growl, too —even scratch, if she's pushed, Stacey thought as she followed Mar and Linda downstairs.

117

Michelle met them at the foot, a towel slung over her shoulder, and eyes sparkling. "Stace! What's up?" she hissed. "We could hear you, clear to the kitchen!"

But Mar silenced her with a shake of her head, led Fritz, Linda, and Stacey into the little-used front room, and closed the door. It was quiet there, with a deep, soft carpet, striped sofa, pillows, and white curtains hanging in folds.

Stacey refused a chair, but planted her feet and listened in scornful silence while Mar told Fritz about her plans for going to Wyoming. "As you see, she made quite a generous offer. . . ."

At first Fritz sat quietly, shaking his head and rubbing his hands over his beard, but before Mar was through, he burst out. "Hey! It's true we need a guide, but we're not that desperate. We can get along. And Stacey is"—he turned toward her—"Stacey . . . you're a really neat kid, but we can't legally hire anybody so young. I wish we could, because you could teach us plenty. But the law's the law."

"Sure. I guess I knew it all along." Stacey felt oddly deflated to find that her Noble Gesture wouldn't work after all.

At this, no longer a tiger-mom but friendly again, Mar smiled and turned toward Fritz. "The solution is actually quite simple. Today is Friday. Linda can help you tomorrow and Sunday, and leave on Monday. Stacey can show you and Penny some new trails almost any time and still have her week in Wyoming. Can you find someone else to take Linda's classes?"

"Sure," Fritz agreed. "They may not be as super as she is, but lots of people are hunting for jobs with horses. I'll call the academy that sent us our other teachers."

"So . . . ." Mar drew a deep breath. "After this—I'm afraid very noisy—tempest in a teapot, can we return to sanity? The first step is for you, Linda, to telephone your Mr. Perry. Do you know how to reach him?"

"He gave all of us his number at the cast party."

"Good. Find out whether the job is still open. If it is, tell him you can leave on Monday and ask him the best route. Train? Bus? I assume it's not the easiest place in the world to get to." She brushed back a strand of her dark hair. "You'll be here to see Penny and Fritz through the weekend, and then they'll have several days between sessions to get someone else started."

"I feel so *dumb*!" Stacey murmured. "All that fuss!"

"Me, too," added Linda. But she was already on the way to the telephone.

There it was quickly decided. No, Mr. Perry hadn't located a suitable replacement, and yes—yes, by all means —Linda must come as soon as she could. He would get in touch immediately with the director at LaRue.

"So . . . ." Fritz hauled himself to his feet. "I'll tell Pen it's all squared away. And I'll see you in the morning,

Linda. If you've any weather-magic, we could use some sunshine to dry out the mud. Papas and mamas, you know." With a wave of his hand, he left, to slosh his way down the hill.

As soon as the door was closed, Michelle beckoned Stacey into a corner of the dining room. "Hey! What was that all about?" she asked in an eager whisper. "You and Lin sounded like a couple of cats on a back fence."

"We had a problem." Stacey tried to salvage a few shreds of dignity. "It's all straightened out now."

"You could tell me!" Michelle flapped the dish towel. "It must have been a really big bust-up."

"Well—the *fight* was just dumb," Stacey began, but as she remembered Linda's trouble with the nail polish, she burst into a laugh. "A couple of cats is right! It must have been really sensational, with both of us yowling at each other. Linnie got scratching mad, so of course I got mad, too." More soberly, she explained what had happened.

Michelle found a dozen questions to ask. "That's the *best.* Positively," she said, when she had it all straight. "I'm going to find Linnie right now and tell her how special it is. Only—she'll be gone pretty soon, and I'll miss her."

I'll miss her, too, Stacey thought. I'll miss her a lot.

As Fritz had hoped, the next day was fine, and on

Sunday—Parents' Day—the mountains stood against the blue sky as if they had been scrubbed, with high rims of glistening snow and the smell of sage sharp on the breeze. Michelle gobbled her breakfast, chattering between bites, then set out for the camp.

By noon she was back. "Come *on!*" she urged Stacey. "The gymkhana's going to be *so neat!* Some of the moms and dads have come already. And Elfrieda and Myrna and Susie and—oh, a whole bunch of kids—have promised to write to me, and Myrna's going to come back next term."

"I hope they have a good time, Mish, and you, too. But . . . ."

"They're going to have a boot race—that's when they put all their boots in a pile and race to the end and find their own and put them on. And an egg race—that's when they ride with eggs in spoons. And a partners' race —that's where one kid rides and his partner has to saddle the horse. And gymnastics—the tricks they've learned in gym. And . . . ."

"Mish, it sounds really great. But you tell me about it afterward, okay? I'm going to give Whisper an extra-good workout, and I have a new book to read."

Although Stacey thought Michelle was gone for the afternoon, just after five o'clock she slammed the kitchen door. "Stace! Hey—*Stace!*"

Stacey, who had finished with Whisper and was in

the breezeway reading *To Kill a Mockingbird,* called out, "Here I am. What's up?"

"It's Victor!" Michelle burst in.

"Is he hurt?" Stacey laid down her book.

"It's his dad! Victor thought he was coming after him, and he got all packed and everything. But instead his father sent word that he can't come. And Stace—he *has to stay for the next session, too.* He can't even go home between terms." Michelle was heaving with indignation.

"Poor little guy!"

"And that's not all. He'll be the only kid down there for almost a whole week. Penny says she doesn't know what they'll do with him. So I thought . . . . Stace, you'd better go. Everybody's left now except him, and he won't come downstairs."

At that instant the kitchen door opened and closed again, and Linda walked in. "Is it true?" Stacey demanded. "Mish says Victor has to stay over."

"Right. Poor little kid."

Michelle pulled off her hat and rubbed her neck, where the chinstrap had left a red mark. "He likes you better than anybody. Penny said so, and Fritz, too. I think you'd better come."

Stacey sighed. "Look . . . I'm sorry he's having a bad time, but what possible reason could I have for butting in?"

Michelle spoke slowly, with exaggerated patience. "This: I told them I'd take him on some neat rides, but they said I'm too young. But they both thought it was a real good idea . . . for you to . . . ."

"Actually, she's right," Linda put in. "You're old enough to be trusted, and you could show him a lot of fun."

Stacey set her jaw. "There are a hundred other things I'd rather do."

"Oh?" asked Linda in her coolest voice. "What about that big-hearted offer you made to Fritz and Penny? Except for that, I'd be staying here to help Victor myself. Were you just grandstanding?"

"I most certainly . . . ." Stacey broke off and stared out the long windows at the mountains, which were veiled now with the ruddy haze of sunset, purple in the valleys, rosy at their peaks. Maybe Linda was right. Maybe she'd been trying to look noble. Only—did she have to take on Victor? For almost a week? That wretched camp was a whirlpool, sucking her in deeper and deeper, and *she didn't want it.*

But then she remembered skinny little Victor, with his enormous brown eyes. "Oh, all right. Let's go. I'll do *something* with him. One ride, anyway."

She found Penny and Fritz sitting side by side on the wooden steps of the boys' dormitory, which seemed oddly quiet with the children gone. Small waves lapped at the shore and a fish jumped, but there were no footsteps, no voices, no laughter. "Catching our breath," Penny explained, as she untied the ribbon that held back her coppery hair. "The last parents just left. You should have come, Stacey. Big day."

"I know it was," Stacey replied. "The reason I'm here now is Victor. Mish says . . . ."

Penny sighed. "Poor little guy. Dumped is the word, I think."

Stacey glanced toward the door. "Is he . . . ?"

"Holed up in his room—and been there all day." Fritz's face was sober. "We've had somebody with him, so he hasn't been alone, but he's going to have a dull time the rest of the week."

"Actually, we had to make room, because our second term was full," Penny added. "We seem to be the only people anywhere that are much interested in him."

Again the memory of Victor, his sneeze, his straggle of hair, swept over Stacey. "What a *horrible* father!" she exclaimed.

Fritz was grinning. "Not very judicious language, Stace, but it's exactly how we feel, too. Only we have to be polite. You'd be surprised how hard that can be." He looked oddly at her. "How about going up to see him? He likes you."

"Okay."

They found Victor sitting on his bed with the youngest counselor, a girl named Nancy, on a chair beside it, and a Parcheesi board between them. "Somebody's come to call, fellow," Fritz announced, then turned to the counselor. "That's enough for now, Nancy, and thanks.

We want some time with this guy, too." He tousled Victor's head.

"That's right," added Penny with a smile. "We missed you today."

The child glanced up at them, but quickly away again, and mumbled, "Hi."

"Hi, Victor. Had a good game?" asked Stacey.

"It was all right." He dumped the pieces on the bed and folded the board. "I beat."

"Good for you." Dropping down beside him, Stacey decided to try a direct approach. "I'm really sorry you couldn't go home."

Victor was carefully arranging the Parcheesi pieces in their box. "My dad wanted to have me. He wrote me a real long letter on his office paper. It was a real nice typed letter. But—my mom—my mom . . . ." He dropped a red counter and scrambled for it under the bed, his voice muffled. "She's getting better. My dad's real glad of that."

"It's wonderful news, Victor. We're all glad."

"And lookit what he sent me." Standing up again and sliding his hand under the pillow, he brought out a miniature blue TV with a three-inch screen. "I can even play it at night, under the . . . ." He glanced at Fritz.

"Under the covers," the tall man finished for him, with a smile. "You'll be the hit of the camp."

"Yeah. It'll be fun, all right."

"Victor," said Stacey, clasping her hands between

her knees. "I'm going to have a lot of time on my hands this week." Oh, yes? she asked herself. What about training Whisper? But she rushed ahead.

"I'd like to take you on some special rides—just you and me and Mish—to a lake I know, and a couple of canyons. Would you like that?"

"Well—maybe."

"Or would you like to visit our barn again?"

"Can I pet the little ones?" Interested but still wary, Victor glanced sidewise at her.

"I think so," Stacey replied. "How about feeding Breeze his bottle?" She noticed that Penny and Fritz were both nodding, evidently pleased.

Victor dropped his TV onto the bed. *"Honest?* Well —sure."

"You'll have to hang on tight, because he's getting strong and he pulls hard."

"Look!" Victor held up his arm and made a fist. "I could hang on, all right."

"Okay. And you can lead him around the stall a little, with me there to help. I tried a halter on him last week, and he didn't mind. But you'll have to do it the way I tell you."

"Sure."

"And only for a few minutes. We mustn't let him get tired."

"I'll be real careful. I'll stop the very *second* you tell me. And . . . my pony?" He turned toward Fritz. "If we go on those rides, can I still have Golden Boy for mine?"

Fritz tousled the child's hair. "Golden Boy has to have time off this week, after all the workouts you gave him. We'll find you another, and when camp starts again, you can have Golden Boy back."

"You can use our Shoebutton," Stacey told him. "I used to ride him, and then Michelle did, and now that we have bigger ones, he's lonesome. He'll be glad to have a rider."

Victor slid off the bed and reached for Stacey's hand. "Sure. I'd like Shoebutton just fine. Anybody ought to be able to handle more than one horse. And say . . . can we go see Breeze right now?

"Okay," she replied, with a glance at Penny, who nodded. "He's already been fed, but you can get acquainted."

He was already leading her out the door. "I expect he'll be real glad to see me."

"I'm sure he will." Stacey followed him downstairs, and they started up the knoll.

10.
Entertaining Victor

---

*It happened so fast—I can't
believe it, even when I look
down the knoll.*
—STACEY'S DIARY
JULY 25

THE MORNING AFTER PARENTS' DAY, Stacey awoke with
a head full of plans: She'd give the horses a really good
brushing, have a special workout with Whisper, and later
on she'd ride up to High Tor and read *To Kill a Mockingbird* beside the lake.

But before she finished her jobs in the barn, she
heard the door creak and Victor came in, closely followed
by Michelle. "Hey, Stacey—is this early enough?" he
asked, stopping outside the stall she was spreading with
fresh straw.

Brandy, who had been dozing in the corner, came over to sniff his hand, and Stacey forced herself to smile. "Early enough for what?" she asked.

"To feed the little one. You said I could." Victor's eyes were big and anxious behind his glasses.

Michelle pushed in front of him. "I explained that we feed him *really early* because he's always so hungry," she blurted. "But he just keeps saying, 'She *told* me I could. . . . She *told* me I could.' So I said let's go ask." She tromped across the floor to Breeze's stall and flung the door open. "See? He isn't even *here.* Just like I said."

"Oh." Victor peered into the empty stall. "I guess you're right. I'm too late."

Stacey leaned the pitchfork against the wall with a thump that jabbed it into the wooden floor. End of peace and quiet! But—poor little guy—there wasn't a single kid at camp for him to play with. "We used to feed Breeze every hour, but he's older now and doesn't need it so often," she said. Then, as Victor shoved his hands into his pockets and turned away, she hastily added, "By the time I finish the stalls it will be nearly noon, and you can give him his bottle then. Okay?"

"Neat!" Victor rubbed his sleeve across his nose. "I'd just as soon wait as not. Say—what are you doing, anyway?"

"Fixing Nutmeg a nice clean bed," Stacey replied, which made Victor laugh.

"A bed! For a horse!"

"That's right. And now . . . ." What could you do with a forlorn little boy who had apparently settled in for the day? "Suppose you sit on the corral fence like a cowhand, while I work Buttermilk on the lunge line."

"I could do Flat Top for you," Michelle suggested. "Shall we go get them, Victor and I? He could lead one back."

"Well—all right," Stacey agreed a bit doubtfully, and they swaggered off together.

For the next hour, Victor sat on the top rail and watched cartoons on his miniature TV, while Stacey and Michelle worked the two-year-olds. Now and then he slid off to pet Brandy, who had adopted a dignified position at his feet. Sometimes he gave a cheer. "Go it, Stacey!" "Faster!"

Before they were through, Tiny appeared, hayfork in hand. "Those geldings are coming along fine," he said with a nod of his long head. "I knew you were a born trainer, Stacey, but Mish here—she is, too. Small package, big person. Plenty of grit."

Stacey glanced at Michelle, little and stocky, tugging at Flat Top's line. "She's doing a good job," she agreed.

"You'll have some real fine horses there, time you're through with them." Tiny pulled out a bandanna and wiped his high forehead. "Ought to bring a top price."

As he left the corral, he stopped to give Victor's knee a friendly slap. "Studying how to be a cowhand, are you?"

"Yep," Victor replied. "I've learned a lot already."

"Good for you." Tiny went back into the barn, and Stacey resumed her patient circling with Huckleberry Finn.

"Hey—who's that?" Victor called.

"Tiny, the man who helps us."

"*Tiny!*" Victor was convulsed with giggles. "He isn't *tiny!*"

"Just a nickname. He's one of our best friends."

After a few more circles, Stacey let Huckleberry Finn loose in the pasture. "Time to feed Breeze. Hop down now," she said, giving Victor her hand.

They filled a bottle at the house, and when they returned, the black colt was waiting by the gate of Brook Meadow, ears pricked and neck arched, with Mr. Lee close by. "Here we are, beautiful!" Stacey said as she slipped the latch. The other horses, who were peacefully grazing, trotted up close.

"There sure are a lot!" exclaimed Victor. "Do you know them all?"

"Sure. That big gelding is Sultan, my dad's. Miranda —the bay mare over there—is the one Mar rides this summer, because Lady Jane is taking care of her baby," Stacey said, and named the rest. "See how they've pricked their ears? They wonder whether we brought them a treat."

"Is that one mine?" Victor asked, pointing toward a Shetland pony who was black all over, with not a white hair showing. "He isn't very big."

"That's Shoebutton, and you'll soon find out that he's big enough," Stacey said.

"What she means is, he's a brat," added Michelle. "Sometimes he's real stubborn."

"Well—I can handle him, all right," Victor confidently replied.

By now Breeze was bunting them and whiffling with impatience, so Stacey led him aside. "Here," she told Victor, "I'll get him started this time, and then you'll know how." She held the bottle, nipple down, until the colt was sucking hard. "Now." One by one she put the child's hands in place. "Hang on tight. He really pulls."

Giggling, Victor clutched the bottle with all his might, while Breeze smacked at it and waggled his tail. "Wow! I didn't think he'd be so strong!"

"He's strong, all right," called Michelle, who was feeding carrots to the other horses. "I dropped it three times, until I learned to really grab on."

"*I* won't drop it," Victor stoutly asserted. But almost at once Breeze tugged it away.

"Never mind," Stacey consoled him. "It didn't break. Just hang on tighter." She picked up the bottle, dusted it off, and helped them get started again.

After petting Breeze and giving Shoebutton a carrot, Victor left for his lunch at camp, but sooner than seemed possible the back door rattled again.

"I hurried!" he announced, breathing fast. "Am I in time for the ride?"

"Plenty of time." Be *nice* to him, be *nice* to him, Stacey told herself. He's lonesome, and it's only for a few days. "Are you going, Mish?" she asked.

"Might as well."

"Okay. Let's saddle up." Stacey put her book and some apples into a bag, and they all trooped out to the barn.

A few minutes later they started for High Tor, Stacey on Whisper Please, Michelle on Tommy Rot, and Victor hanging gamely to Shoebutton's saddle horn. As she watched him bounce along, Stacey remembered her own struggles with Shooey's rough trot, and she slowed Whisper to a walk. "There's a lake up there, but it's pretty far," she said. "Are your legs strong enough?"

"They're strong, all right. I'd like a real long ride. Shooey would, too."

"And part of the trail is scary."

"I'm never scared." Later, when they skirted a ledge, Victor took one look at the drop-off, shut his eyes, and grabbed Shooey's mane, but pressed his lips together and rode in silence. Tough little kid, Stacey thought.

Their path wound between hummocks and rocks and gradually climbed, with the land below spreading wider as they rose, until it lay like the open pages of a book: wheat fields, the ragged Bend with Cat Creek looping around it, and Fox Lake, bordered with pines. Whisper pressed eagerly forward, waggling her ears and snuffling from time to time as if she, too, enjoyed the trek.

Stacey was in the lead with Victor next and Michelle at the rear, calling out directions: "It's all right, Victor. Shooey knows how to go," or "Hey! Let go your saddle horn. Relax."

At last they were on High Tor, Stacey's favorite mountain meadow, with a tiny lake in the center, and half a dozen miniature streams that zigzagged in every direction, edged with flowers. "Monkey faces," she identified the yellow ones, which made Victor laugh. "Penstemon —these blue ones beside the rocks. And honeysuckle."

She took the apples out of her saddlebag—one each for the people, one each for the horses—then pulled out her book and began to read, while Michelle and Victor gathered worms in the marshy ground at the end of the lake. Blackbirds were singing in the reeds. The sun was warm. When they resaddled their horses and started back, Stacey realized that, even with Victor, it had been a perfect ride.

Before they had finished breakfast the next morning, he was at the door again, carrying a sack. "Penny sent my lunch, so I can stay a real long time," he said, beaming through his glasses.

"Well." Stacey tried not to show her dismay. "We have some work to do first, but then—how about looking for petroglyphs?"

"Pet—pedri—what did you say?"

"Pet-ro-glyphs," Stacey slowly repeated. "They're old, old pictures, carved on the rocks. Maybe you'd like to make some rubbings?"

"*Rubbings? On rocks?*"

Stacey smiled. "It's a way of copying them. Want to try?"

"Oh, boy! Neat!" He perched on the corral fence with his miniature TV, until the girls were ready to go.

This time they went to Lava Bend, and as they wove their way along, Stacey pointed out the rock formations they passed: Big Bear; the Castle; the Giant's Pipe Organ. At the lip of the canyon where Rod Wright had shown them his petroglyph, Mish shook her fist at it and scowled, but Victor didn't see.

They rode into a ravine where several small carvings were low on the rocks, and there Victor bit his lips, and rubbed, and rubbed again, until he had copied a mountain sheep.

"I wish we could make some more," he said, as Stacey rolled his pages up to tie behind his saddle. "I want to show them to my mom—when she's better."

"We'll try," Stacey agreed.

The rest of the week flashed by, doing things with Victor, always with Victor. On Wednesday morning they had a "circus" in which Stacey jumped onto Whisper's back—stood up—slid off over her rump and climbed on the same way. She threw down an apple and when Whisper bent her head to pick it up, she slid off down her neck. Michelle spun twice on Tommy's back and somersaulted off.

In the afternoon Gwen rode over for another practice around the barrels, after which they all went together to let Victor catch tadpoles in the Ox-Eye Meadow pond.

Thursday afternoon they explored a cave in Plunder Gorge. On the way back they glimpsed the surveyor Stacey's father had hired to search with metal detectors for the iron boundary pipes. "Dad," Stacey asked in the evening. "Did he find—?"

Her father shook his head. "Nothing, so far. He's still looking."

Just then the telephone rang and Linda was on the line. "Summer stock is terrific—really super," she said. "I'm learning so much. . . . I love you all—Mar and Dad and everybody. And I hardly have time to breathe."

Sooner than seemed possible, it was Friday, the beginning of the second session, when Victor would be busy again at camp. Stacey had been counting the days, but now she found herself listening for his rattle at the door. "How are the new kids, Mish? Pretty nice?" she asked.

Michelle gave her braids a flip. "Why—sure. Don't tell me you're *worrying* about that *horrible camp*!"

"Just about Victor."

Michelle grinned. "I thought you hated everybody down there."

"Not Victor! Or Penny and Fritz. Now that I know them . . . well. . . ."

"You like them just fine," Michelle finished for her. "That's exactly what I kept telling you. They have lots of neat people, if you'd give them a chance."

Stacey turned away. "It's our ranch, and we've lived here forever, and I don't want it all cluttered up."

"Well. You can't have it, and *not* have it, both at once." Michelle shrugged. "Me, I like it fine."

Although Stacey resolutely stayed away from camp that weekend, Michelle kept the family informed. She had met "a whole bunch of kids." She was to take swimming lessons with the Minnows instead of the Tadpoles. Linda's replacement had come and was "pretty good— but not as good as Linnie."

"Have you seen Victor?" Stacey asked, reminding herself that she didn't really care.

Michelle nodded. "He's in trouble. Penny and Fritz grounded him because he and another boy ran off."

Stacey was surprised at her own reaction. Victor had run off again—and she was pleased. At last he'd found a friend.

Sunday afternoon was hot, just right for stretching out in the hammock with a book and a Coke, but the sky was hard and blue, the poplar leaves quivering, and a ball of tumbleweed rolled past. Before long Stacey retreated inside because the wind was stirring up so much dust.

She settled uneasily in her favorite chair in the family room, while Suds whined and pattered from window to window.

Jeff was troubled, too. "I don't like this wind," he told Stacey just before bedtime. "Let's get the horses, especially the foals, under cover."

"Sure," she replied, and helped them into the barn.

She hurried to bed, but lay awake for a long time with her thoughts in a muddle. Victor's mother . . . Rod Wright . . . her father, who had looked so tired today. He tried not to let it show, but he was worried.

When at last she fell asleep, it seemed only moments until something startled her awake. Brandy—why was he barking like that? And who was shouting? With a vague idea that she was having a nightmare, she struggled to a sitting position and had just set foot to the rug when someone banged on her door.

"Stacey! Quick!" It was her father's voice.

"What's happened?"

"Fire. Put on your boots and get to the barn! We've got to move the horses."

Fire! She snapped wide awake. With trembling hands she pulled on her jeans, grabbed a light jacket, and raced downstairs. Through the hall—the dining room—the family room. Out the back door, where she had a clear view down the knoll. And there was a flicker of flame, now dim, now bright, in the window of the loft.

In the faint light she could see Brandy running back

and forth, and the dark figures of people—her father? Jeff? Mar?

"I'm coming! I'm coming!" she gasped as she plunged down the path. The fire was growing and spreading, brighter already, burning in hay. And Whisper, her darling Whisper, was shut up in her stall.

11.
Missing!

*It was awful. I was even
more frightened than when I
first heard them holler fire.*
—STACEY'S DIARY
JULY 25

GASPING, STACEY BUTTONED HER JACKET and ran down
the path. If only she and Jeff hadn't put the horses inside!
They were in a hundred times more danger now than they
would have been from a little wind. They knew it, too.
She could hear their frantic neighs, all mixed up with
Brandy's barks.

She reached the barn—ran through the door—
looked into the first stall. And there was Jeff, grabbing for
Sultan's halter while the big bay gelding tossed his head
and snorted. He reared. Jeff jumped—caught the chin

strap. Sultan shook him off and banged both forefeet on the floor.

"Jeff!" Stacey screamed. "He'll trample you."

Without turning around, Jeff leaped and caught the strap again. "You get the rest. I'll handle Sultan," he shouted, just as Michelle came pounding through the door, in pajamas and boots.

"Tommy!" She tripped and almost fell. "Tommy— Tommy! Where are you?" She raced on down the aisle.

Stacey could hear Whisper's hoofs pounding the wall. "Easy, girl. You'll be all right." She flung open the stall door and, heedless of the flailing feet, ran boldly in. "Come along now!"

She grabbed the halter, but Whisper jerked away.

"Come along, I said. Come . . . *Whisper!* You've *got* to come!" She grabbed the halter again, and again the horse jerked free.

Something flashed through Stacey's mind, something her father had once said. *They're afraid to leave their stalls in a fire, because they think they're safe there. They have to be taken out by force.* "So . . . I'll force you," Stacey shouted. "Whisper! *You come!"*

She seized the cheek strap. Pulled it hard. Gave Whisper's neck a whack with the flat of her hand. *"Come, I told you!"* she yelled at the top of her lungs.

All at once Whisper lowered her head and took a cautious step forward. She trembled—pulled back—hesitated—moved forward again. With a sudden, terrible, high-pitched scream, she dashed down the aisle, while Stacey clung to the halter and ran beside her as fast as she could go. They were out the door. Halfway to the corral. Through its gate—and Whisper was safe.

Jeff's Cherokee was there already, prancing and snorting, and Michelle with Tommy Rot.

"Mish!" Stacey's father shouted. "Get them down to the far end! Keep them there. Brandy will help." Stacey heard Michelle yell to the dog and glimpsed him running and barking frantically, with his head thrown back.

Out here the fire seemed closer. From high above came the sharp crackle of flames, flickering through the loft window and casting an eerie glow. Horses were pounding back and forth in the corral, tossing their heads and squealing, while Brandy barked, and Michelle flapped her arms and yelled.

"Fire! Man's worst enemy! Man's best friend!" said a deep voice behind Stacey.

"Tiny!"

"Heard the commotion." Wearing boots and a long white nightshirt, partly stuffed into his trousers, Tiny went flapping like a big bird through the wide-open barn door.

Shooey's still in there . . . Mr. Lee . . . and Lady Jane . . . Stacey thought, as she ran back into the barn and down the aisle to Shoebutton's stall, the farthest one.

He was there, a black smudge in the dimness, whinnying and pawing the floor.

"Easy! It's all right!" Stacey caught his halter and gave it a hard pull. He jerked away. "Come along." Why did her voice squeak so? "Come on, Shooey. Come *on!* You—you *stubborn-heels!*" She pulled as hard as she could. "It's all right. *All right,* I tell you. *Please,* Shooey, come *on!*" And at last Shoebutton lowered his head and followed her into the aisle.

Mar was just ahead, leading her Miranda at a trot. "Run!" she shouted. They raced down the aisle, but a pitchfork had fallen, and Shooey tripped over its handle. He stumbled and fell to his knees.

"Shooey! Get *up!*" Stacey screamed, jerking on his brow band. She hauled him to his feet. He squealed. Tossed his head. Ran again, following Stacey through the door. She opened the corral gate and shoved him through, with a sharp slap on the rump.

"Careful, now," Mar called as they ran back together. "Check for smoke. If you smell any—stay out."

"Right!"

They darted inside, where it was dim, not yet red with fire. Stacey sniffed. The air was fresh, the smoke overhead in the loft. Thankfully she remembered that the hay was in bales, and slower burning than if it were loose. She'd make one more dash.

Halfway down the aisle, she ducked into a stall as Jeff

and her father came along full speed, with Sultan thundering between them, snorting and tossing his head. Both of them were clutching his halter. "Mr. Lee!" Jeff shouted as they passed. "Get him out!"

She looked into a stall—empty. Another—empty. Into Mr. Lee's stall—and he stood valiantly braced across the far corner, shielding Breeze, who was almost out of sight behind the broad back. *Can I do it?* Stacey wondered. *Mr. Lee's so big!*

She grabbed his chin strap. "Come along, sir. *Come along!*" she screamed, and led him a few steps. But he stopped at the stall door and planted his enormous feet, every inch of his big frame trembling.

"Mr. Lee! I don't want to leave you here!" she yelled. "And I *won't.*" Sobbing, she snatched a rope from a nearby peg and gave him a lick with it. He jerked, but stood like a rock. Another lick, using every ounce of her strength. "I can't move you. You're too *big,*" she sobbed. *"Please,* Mr. Lee."

"Tears won't help," said Tiny's voice behind her. "You've got to show them who's boss." Taking her rope, he slipped it through the halter ring. "Now, sir. *Git moving!*" Stacey had never heard Tiny roar so! With a mighty jerk on the rope, he whacked the big horse—who turned all at once and followed meekly into the aisle. "Give the colt a slap, unless he comes, too," Tiny ordered, as he stretched his long legs into a run.

But Breeze didn't want to be left behind. With one

high, frightened, baby nicker, he put his nose close to Mr. Lee's rump and ran, out of the stall and down the aisle, to the corral and safety. "Good fellow," murmured Stacey, as Tiny slapped Mr. Lee's ponderous shoulder and turned him loose. "Tiny—I couldn't have done it if you hadn't come along."

"Takes muscle," was all Tiny replied.

The flames were brighter now. "Nobody's to go in again," said Mar, who was standing beside them. "Anyway, we've got the horses out. All of them, I think. And the people are safe."

Drawing big breaths of the fresh, cool air, Stacey checked through the family. Dad . . . Mar . . . Michelle . . . Jeff . . . Tiny. Everybody was there.

And the horses? Lighted by the eerie, red glow of flames, they were milling in a terrified circle at the far side of the corral, with Brandy running back and forth in front of them, barking his loudest, keeping them together. Quickly Stacey counted them over: Whisper. Lady Jane and her foal. Mr. Lee and Breeze. Dad's Sultan. Linda's Nutmeg. Jeff's Cherokee. Tommy Rot. Shoebutton. Miranda. They were all there, too.

But the barn—! Its walls were black against the flames, which were tossing now like bright streamers above the roof. Even though a fire truck was coming down the road at last, its siren screeching louder every second, Stacey was sure there was no hope. Nothing could put out a fire like this.

Disconsolately the family led the frightened horses one by one into the pasture, well away from the choking clouds of smoke. Then they gathered in a melancholy group and watched the firemen unroll their hose and pour chemicals on the other farm buildings, to keep the fire from spreading. It roared, loud as a train. The roof of the barn collapsed with a crash, sending up a storm of sparks.

Tiny was close to Stacey, his nightshirt now well tucked in. Close to her ear, in his usual calm, melancholy voice, he chanted:

" 'From Brig o' Dread when thou may'st pass,
　　—Every nighte and alle,
　To that great fire thou com'st at last;
　　And Christe receive thy saule.' "

Stacey felt her skin prickle. It always made her feel that way when Tiny recited.

By dawn the barn walls had fallen in, heaped into a smoldering mass of wood.

"Insurance?" the fire chief asked Stacey's father.

"Covered." His face was streaked with soot, his hands were black, and his words came in labored jerks. "But nothing . . . can compensate me for. . . ."

"True." The fire chief rubbed his grimy hands together. "Any idea how it started?"

Stacey's father shook his head. "Not a glimmer. Spontaneous combustion of the hay, I suppose . . . although the weather . . . was it that hot? I just don't know."

"Any suspicious characters around?"

"Haven't seen any."

"Enemies?"

Stacey's father set his lips in a thin line. "If you're thinking of arson . . . no. It wasn't that. Even if I had enemies—which I don't—who would be low enough to set a fire in a horse barn?"

Except Rod Wright? Stacey wondered. Was Rod that low?

"Well, we'll leave a squad here to keep watch until we're sure it's safe, and soon as it's cooled down, we'll investigate. You'd be surprised how much we can figure out, sometimes," the fire chief replied, pulling a notebook out of his pocket. "I'm real sorry about this, Chambers. It's a tough break. We were licked before we started, though. Not much chance, with a loft half full of hay."

"I understand." Stacey's father stared at the blackened timbers. "And thanks for saving the other buildings. I don't see how you. . . ."

"Dad! Mar!" Everybody whirled as Michelle came screeching around the smoldering barn. "Lookit! *Lookit* what I *found!*" She skidded to a stop. "It was just there. . . ." She pointed toward the front of the barn. "On the *ground.* Outside the barn door. Just *lying* there." She handed Mar a small, sooty object.

"*Victor's!*" Mar gasped.

It was a miniature TV.

"It's his, all right," Michelle replied. "He carries it every place he goes."

"Did you see him yesterday?" asked Mar. "Stacey . . . was he here?"

Stacey shook her head. "I don't think so. If he'd been anywhere around, he'd have wanted to feed Breeze."

The fire chief looked up from his notebook, suddenly alert. "Who's Victor?" he asked.

"One of the children from the camp."

"I'd better check it out." The chief closed his book with a snap and reached for the TV. "How do I get there?"

"Over the knoll," Stacey's father replied. "I'll show you." The men strode rapidly away.

Could Victor have come again? Stacey asked herself. *Could he have been in the barn?* Trying not to think about it, she ran after her father and the chief, with Michelle puffing along behind.

The sun was still below the horizon as they climbed the knoll and strode toward the camp. They heard a clamor of voices from inside the boys' dormitory, and when Stacey's father pounded on the door, Fritz came out at once. "Chambers! A rough break! Can I do anything to help?" he asked.

"We've a question," the fire chief said. "I see the fire has pretty thoroughly aroused you folks."

"The kids went wild when they heard the sirens," Fritz replied. "Came pouring down the stairs, hollering that they wanted to go watch. But we've got them corraled in the dining hall, with gallons of hot chocolate, to keep them out of harm's way."

The fire chief sounded grim. "I hope you succeeded," he said, and handed Fritz the tiny TV. "We found this by the barn. Have you called the roll?"

Fritz stared. "Called the roll! Do you mean . . . ?" He turned the TV over in his hand. "We didn't even think of it. We'd had our usual check at bedtime, the kids were all in bed—we thought—when it started, and we've kept a close watch on them. But I'll do it, right now." He flung the door open. "Come inside." He showed them into the common room and disappeared.

Stacey's father walked to the window and stood looking out, with his hands behind his back, while the fire chief held his notebook in his palm, scribbling fast.

"Stace! I'm scared!" whispered Michelle.

"I am, too," Stacey replied. She folded her arms tightly across her stomach, because it kept plunging toward her boots. Why did a simple roll call take so long?

After an eternity the door opened again, and Fritz was there, shoulders sagging and face white behind its beard.

"We've checked, as you suggested. One kid didn't answer, so we looked in his room, and the other rooms, too. He isn't here."

"His name?"

Fritz looked hard at Stacey, and she knew what he was going to say. "It's Victor."

12.
The Search

*I thought Whisper would do it
—or at least I hoped she
would. It was our only chance.*
—STACEY'S DIARY
JULY 25

"WE'LL HAVE SEARCH PARTIES out within an hour," the
fire chief told Fritz and Penny, as they conferred with
him and Stacey's father in the camp's common room.
"National Guard and Girl and Boy Scouts to comb every
trail, starting with the most dangerous ones, in the hills.
And my men will check out the barn—what's left of it—
as soon as it's cool enough."

Michelle gave Stacey a poke. "Stace! Does he
mean—?" she whispered.

"I think so. But that doesn't make it true," Stacey

151

whispered back. "Mish, where did you find that TV?"

"Outside the barn door, in the path."

"So it wasn't in the barn." Stacey pulled her sister aside and whispered. "Mish . . . listen . . . they're talking about the mountains. But Victor wouldn't go there."

"Why not?"

"Because he's scared of heights. Remember when we took him to High Tor?"

Michelle looked at her, wide eyed. "Sure! He kept shutting his eyes and hanging onto Shooey's mane."

"That's right. He liked the *canyons*. And he could find them on the Bend, even at night."

"Was there any moonlight?" Michelle was also whispering.

"Some. Enough to get around by."

Michelle nodded. "We'd better tell them."

"Right." Stacey moved close to Fritz and plucked at his sleeve. "Fritz! Hey—*Fritz!* We've got an idea. We think Victor. . . ."

Fritz brushed her off like a troublesome fly. "Later, Stacey. Right now we're busy."

"But, Fritz—you ought to. . . ."

"Stacey!" Fritz hardly looked at her. "Let's just cool it. Okay? The chief knows this area, and he'll see that every possible place is searched, the most dangerous ones first. He'll handle it better than we can."

"But. . . ."

Fritz frowned and turned his back, giving the chief all his attention.

"Come on, Mish," whispered Stacey. "We'll look for ourselves."

"Right. And hurry up!" Michelle darted toward the door, but Stacey waited long enough to touch her father's elbow.

"Dad—Mish and I are going out on our own."

"Fine." His eyes were on the chief. "Be careful."

"We will. Don't worry about us," Stacey assured him, and followed Michelle out the door.

The cool air of dawn hovered over them, soft with the hushed calm of early morning. A meadowlark sang its liquid song. A fish jumped in the lake.

"I think Victor got scared and ran," Stacey began, as they hurried along. "And that's when he dropped his TV."

"Sure! He's always been a sneak—hiding in our loft. Figuring out ways to see Breeze. Running off is just exactly what he would do! I'll bet he isn't far." Michelle pushed her dark hair away from her face and drew a deep, swelling breath. "Let's get going. I'm ready."

Stacey glanced at her—booted, a rip in her pajama elbow, with soot on her face and hair in a tangle. "Well, you don't exactly look it, but I guess I don't, either. We'll take Whisper and Tommy." She turned toward the camp stables.

"Hey! That's the wrong way!"

Stacey sighed. "Mish—*trust* me! Our tack is all burned up. Remember? We have to at least get bridles, and where else can we do it? Nobody will care. Part of the camp gear belongs to the ranch, anyway." She broke into a run with Michelle close behind.

Most of the horses were outside and the camp barn was quiet, filled with the heavy smell of animals and leather and feed. Going into the oversized tack room, the girls began to hastily paw through racks of gear—saddles lying on horizontal supports and bridles hanging from pegs, tagged with horses' names.

"These are for ponies—the horse ones are over there," said Michelle, who had obviously been in the tack room before. "Stardust—he's so teeny his gear's too small, and so is Laddy's." She moved along the row. "And Tommy would hate a bit with such a long shank . . . but here—Rascal's is about right."

The girls hastily selected equipment and started up the knoll.

From its top they could see their barn, a heap of blackened, smoking timbers, still glowing red in the center. The burned, acrid smell of fire prickled Stacey's nose, and she tried to look the other way.

Although the horses were generally easy to catch, today they laid back their ears and skittered to the far end of the pasture, where they huddled together, tossing their heads and snuffling.

"I wish we had a bucket of oats," said Stacey as she walked steadily forward and held out her hands. "Whisper! *Please!* Come here! Come, girl."

Whisper whinnied and rolled her eyes.

"It's all right—all right." Talking in her softest voice and moving a few inches at a time, Stacey drew near enough to touch Whisper's shoulder, and in another moment she had a hand on the halter.

As soon as Whisper was caught, Tommy Rot came bravely forward, and the girls began to adjust the borrowed bridles, lengthening some straps and shortening others. When the brow band, even at its tightest notch, hung loose, Stacey took it completely off. Leading Whisper to a sizable rock, she mounted from there, and by then Michelle was ready, too.

They started bareback toward the Bend. The only sounds were the plop of hoofs, the crunch of dry twigs underfoot, and the morning songs of wrens and meadowlarks. Glancing back, Stacey saw a rolling column of smoke above the knoll, gray against the sky, and she quickly looked away again. A few minutes later when they rounded the shoulder of the Giant's Pipe Organ, even the smoke was out of sight.

"Are we going any special place?" asked Michelle.

Stacey sighed. "Victor doesn't know one canyon from another."

"Crimeny! Do we look in them all?"

"Maybe. It depends on luck."

They jogged on. Even here on the quiet Bend the horses were nervous. When a rabbit bounded out from underfoot, Tommy Rot shied and started to run, snorting and tossing his head until Michelle pulled him to a halt. When a magpie skittered along in front of them, dragging its long black tail, Whisper trembled and neighed.

Before long they came to a shallow ravine with an easy downward slope. At the bottom the girls slid off, dropped the reins, and started their search on foot, pulling at brush and looking behind rocks.

"Victor!" they shouted. "It's all right! Nobody was hurt! Holler if you hear us." Only an echo replied, and they were soon stopped by sheer rock walls.

"So—this isn't the one," Stacey decided. They returned the way they had come, climbed the slope, and jogged on again.

The second ravine was smaller than the first, quickly searched and rejected.

The third was deeper, with a muddy stream at the bottom where the horses had a drink. Along the rim were vertical columns of rock, several of which had small petroglyphs. "This is where Victor made his rubbing," Stacey said. "He copied the antelope over there, and he wanted that bigger one, but it was too high."

"He liked those caves, too." Michelle was looking at some black holes on the cliff. "Remember? He said he'd like to live in a cave. If he's in one now, he'll be really hard to find."

They searched the canyon upstream and down until they were stopped by impassable rocks. Leaving it, they searched another, calling Victor's name. The sun was higher now, shining into the canyon depths and casting black shadows beneath the chaparral, and still they plunged through thickets and pulled aside brush, until Stacey felt as if she had been there forever. Occasionally they saw petroglyphs, which Stacey vaguely planned to come back and copy someday, but her only real concern was Victor, so little and frail and alone.

"I'm thirsty!" Michelle exclaimed as they entered another fairly deep canyon, with a stream that was edged by willow trees. "And this water is the color of mud. Do you think it's fit to drink?"

"Better not. Victor couldn't have come much farther, so we'll have to go back pretty soon, and you can get a Coke then." Stacey patted Whisper's neck, which was glistening with sweat. "I'm sorry, pretty girl. You're just as hot as I am, and this trek isn't much fun for either of us."

They walked along the stream, leading their horses. Stacey was wondering whether it was really worthwhile when she heard a sound that seemed to come from an especially thick stand of willow. "Mish!" She stood still. And there it was again! "It's Victor's sneeze!"

"I heard it, too," Michelle whispered back. "S-s-sh."

It came again, louder this time, and they tied their horses, then plunged into the thicket, heedless of whiplike branches that caught on their clothes and pulled their hair. "Victor!" Stacey called. "Where are you? Come out."

Did she hear a voice?

"You might as well show yourself," she continued. "I'm not going to quit."

The voice again, not quite so faint this time, and the girls pushed still deeper into the brush.

"Crimeny!" Michelle exclaimed, as a stiff branch ripped at the hole in her sleeve. "Do you think he crawled into this?"

"He might have," Stacey replied. "I wish we'd brought an ax."

They heard another sneeze.

"It came from up there—I think!" Michelle said, staring toward the canyon wall. And. . . ." She tore off a larger branch. "Stacey! There he is."

Pulling herself through the gap Michelle had made, Stacey found herself in a small, clear space like a room, with the cliff on one side and willows all the rest of the way around. She followed Michelle's pointing finger. And there was Victor, clinging like a frightened bird to a ledge on the canyon wall, a ledge that was decidedly higher than their heads. *"Victor!"* she exclaimed. "You come right down."

He stared solemnly back. "I . . . I can't!" he whispered, his face scarlet in the hot sun. "It's too far."

Stacey pulled a tangle of leaves from her hair. "You —you little dope!" she exclaimed. "Climbing a place you can't come down from. What got into you, anyway?"

"I was going to hide. In that cave." He jerked his head at a black hole above him. "And then. . . ." He sneezed and wiped his nose on his sleeve. "I've been here an awful long time."

"Well, don't jump off now. You'll get hurt. Just wait a bit, and we'll figure out a way."

She surveyed the cliff. She could see how he'd climbed it, because its face had plenty of handholds and toeholds. She could also guess why he was frightened, because it was always harder to go down than up, and the wall was steep. She had to help him, somehow, but even if she climbed to his ledge, she wouldn't have anything to hang onto while she gave him a hand down. And he couldn't jump, because it would be as dangerous as jumping out of an upstairs window. "Let me think," she said.

She looked over the rock again—not a shrub to cling to.

She looked up—nothing to catch a rope, even if she had one to throw.

She examined the ground—no hummocks, no logs. Nothing to stand on. Plenty of rocks, but the big ones would be too heavy to move. The willow they had fought their way through was a growth of enormous bushes rather than a single tree, the branches growing upright like huge fans. Their bark was smooth to touch and free of thorns, but they were too far from the rock for Victor to reach.

"Shall we tell him to jump and try to catch him?" whispered Michelle at her elbow.

"And have him land on those rocks? Suppose he hit his head?"

"Crimeny. It might kill him." Michelle tore off another branch. "I wish I had Tommy in here, so I could stand on his back."

"Nervous as he is? Remember, he's just been through a fire." They could hear the horses outside the thicket, stamping their feet now and then, and nickering.

"I think he'd stand, if you held his halter. I'd be pretty high."

"And what next? Have Victor leap into your arms, and both go down in a heap? You'd bash out your brains!"

"Oh. Well . . . I guess it wouldn't work."

Stacey thought it through again. "But, Mish, you've given me an idea. I'm going to bring Whisper in here—she's older than Tommy and steadier, and she's taller, too. I'm going to coax her close to the tree . . . there, the one with those longest, skinny branches . . . and stand on her back. . . . Yes! That'll work. I'll bend down that biggest branch—willow's always limber, and it's good and long. And. . . ."

"I don't know . . . she's awful big, to squeeze through!"

"We'll make her a path." Stacey began to break off willow shoots, grabbing them with both hands.

"It's going to scrape her sides. She'll be scared, especially right after the fire. Besides, what good will it do, even if you get her in here?"

"Just *help!* Don't waste time talking."

"I could go get Fritz or Jeff, while you stay with Victor."

Stacey stood up and put her hands on her hips. *"Honestly! Mish!* Look at him! No water! Red as a beet! Suppose he falls off! He's just about had it, with the sun beating down on that ledge. Just *stop complaining* and do it my way." With a sharp snap she laid flat a larger branch. "You hang tight, Victor," she called. "We'll hurry. And then you'll have to help yourself some."

"Sure. I can do that, all right."

"So—here goes." With a resounding *thwack*, Stacey broke the largest branch she could reach, then tore it back until it came free. If Whisper hadn't been too frightened by the fire—if she would come through the brush—and stand. . . . She *had* to. It was all up to Whisper now.

13.
Stacey Remembers

*Just as if a curtain had gone
up, I suddenly knew what had
been bugging me.*

—STACEY'S DIARY
JULY 25

STACEY WORKED FRANTICALLY at the willow brush while Mish wriggled through to the outside and tackled it from there. Most of the shoots in this part of the thicket were not very large, so the girls tore some off and broke others partway through, laying them flat.

"We're getting it, Victor," Stacey called from time to time. Her hands were scraped; she broke a fingernail. "You stay there and try not to worry."

She snapped another branch. "Are you okay, Mish?"

"Sure. But crimeny—I wish I had some gloves."

Michelle's voice sounded near, and when Stacey flattened one more stem, she saw her sister's face, grinning at her through the leaves. "Hi! We did it!" Michelle exclaimed. "Just like engineers, meeting in a tunnel."

Stacey stood up and flexed her arms, looking back, then forward, along their path. As Michelle said, it was a tunnel, and although it had seemed long while they were making the trail, it was quite short after all. The rough ground, covered with crisscrossed branches, would frighten any horse, for they always want to protect their feet. But with Michelle to help, she thought she could coax Whisper through.

She picked her way to the outside, where their animals were nibbling at a patch of bunch grass. "Now, Beautiful, please trust me. You're a darling." She took hold of the reins close to Whisper's chin, and the mare willingly followed her to the entrance of the tunnel. But there she planted her feet and refused to budge. "Easy, girl. It isn't far." Stacey kept up a gentle tug on the reins. "Just a few steps. Come along."

Whisper set her teeth and laid back her ears.

"I'll get some grass," said Michelle, and gathered a large handful.

"Thanks," said Stacey, and held it close to the horse's nose, talking softly, until Whisper took a trembling step.

"Good girl! A little farther now." Stacey kept talking and pulling on the reins, and Whisper moved ahead, one step at a time. In a few minutes they stopped in the little clearing close to the tallest willows and opposite Victor's rock.

"Now, Victor, while Mish holds Whisper steady, I'm going to stand on her back, so I can reach that biggest branch and pull it down to you," Stacey declared, pulling off her boots. With the help of the willows, she managed to grab the mane and scramble up. "And now, Pretty girl —*please!* If you ever stood still in your life, this is the time."

She patted Whisper's sweaty neck and talked about anything or nothing until the mare was quiet, while Michelle, at her head, kept a firm hold on the reins. "Now, if I can stand up. . . ." Slowly, steadying herself by the nearest trees, Stacey pulled herself erect and curled her toes against the furry back. Whisper was trembling beneath her, but she held firm. "You love," Stacey told her. "You know you're doing something special."

She looked up at the willow, whose long arms were small enough to be limber, but large enough to be strong. "Don't be scared, Victor," she called. "Whisper's used to letting me do tricks."

"I know. You showed me," he replied in a tiny voice.

"So—here we go!" Stacey stretched up, feeling teetery—and yes! She could reach a small sprig of the main branch.

In slow motion she drew the sprig toward her, which bent the main stem slightly down. With her other hand she caught a larger sprig—and another—drawing the main bough lower each time until she had it in a firm grip.

"Victor, I'm going to pull this away down," she said. "As soon as it's close enough, you take tight hold and then go across hand over hand—the same as you do in the gym."

"Uh-uh!" Victor wiped his sleeve across his nose. "I'm scared!"

"Maybe so, but you're brave, too. Be sure you get hold of the main branch every time, not a little one."

"Well. . . ."

"It isn't very far, and I'll hang on, so it won't fly up. We'll count and see how many handholds it takes. And in a minute you'll be in the tree." She forced a smile. "I know you can climb trees, Victor. Remember that night in our barn?"

With frightened brown eyes, he stared at the swaying cluster of leaves. He reached a timid hand toward them, but drew it back. "I might slip."

Stacey was sure she'd never been more uncomfortable in her life, perched on Whisper, trying to cling with her toes, her arms stretched high overhead, and her fingers beginning to ache. "Victor Edward McCauley! I'm scared, too, and I've scraped half the skin off my hands!" she exclaimed. "You got yourself into this! Now get yourself out. You're good at gym—Fritz told me. So . . . right hand first."

"O-o-oh!" He grabbed a stem, and another, but

finally caught the main one, gave a panicky little moan, and swung off the ledge. The branch bent under his weight, and he hung there, thin legs dangling.

Wow! Stacey thought. He's pretty far from the ground. But in her most cheerful voice she said, "Good boy. That's handhold number one. Now, move your right just a little—and the left next to it—that's two. And now the right again. Take time to get a good tight grip!"

"Three! . . . Four! . . ." Victor gasped. "Sure! I c'n . . . do it!" Panting, he edged himself monkey-fashion toward the tree, while Stacey and Michelle counted with him.

When he reached Stacey, she helped him swing past, keeping her own hands out of his way. "I can't lift you down—I'm too teetery," she told him. "It's all I can do to hold the willow steady. Just keep going. Six . . . seven."

"I c'n do it!" Victor's legs were swinging as he moved along. In another moment he reached the tree and gave a yell of triumph.

"And *there you are!* You're *wonderful!*" Stacey exclaimed.

"I'll say," shouted Michelle.

Slipping, breaking off leaves, Victor climbed to the ground. "I guess I did that, all right!" he crowed. "I guess I really hung on!"

"I guess you did," Stacey agreed, sliding off over Whisper's rump. "You're a tough little cookie, Victor.

I'm proud of you." Breathing hard, she sat on the ground and pulled on her boots.

"I guess my dad will be proud of me, too, when he finds out what I did. I guess he'll. . . ." Victor broke off. "Do you think he'll tell me this was pretty good?"

"I'm sure of it," Stacey promised. "Now—we have to get Whisper out of here and take you back to camp." Why did she feel like crying, when Victor was safe? Because he was such a plucky little guy? But there wasn't time for tears, so she jumped to her feet and went to Whisper's head. "I'll take her now. You help Victor," she said to Michelle.

"Aw, this is easy." He swaggered through the tunnel, with Michelle at his heels.

Stacey patted Whisper's neck and made ready to follow them. "Steady—you're all right. Turn around. One foot—another. . . ." Slowly she coaxed the frightened mare to the open floor of the canyon, where she flung her arms around Whisper's neck. "I knew you would do it! I knew it!"

After planting a kiss on the velvety nose, she turned toward Michelle. "And you too, Mish. You were super! Toughest little sister in the whole United States!"

"Crumb-bum!" Michelle replied. "I was scared stiff."

"Me too!" Stacey replied. "Now, Victor, I'll help you aboard, and you can have a nice ride home. Hang onto the mane, tight as you can." She led Whisper up the gradual ascent to the Bend, then mounted in front of Victor.

He sat quietly, clutching her waist. "Victor," she said, after a few minutes. "We found your TV. Why did you go to the barn again, when you'd promised not to?"

He didn't answer.

"Did you have matches? I should think you'd know better than that," she persisted.

Victor drew a shuddery breath. "I know better, all right. It was really dumb." He hesitated. "Did all of the barn burn up?"

"Every bit."

"I'm—it was dumb, all right. What d'you think my dad will say?"

"Well—he'll probably ask some questions. But he won't be very cross, because he'll be so glad you weren't hurt."

Victor sneezed and rubbed his nose across her back.

Because it was so hot and Whisper was carrying double, they let the horses walk. "We ought to have a gun and fire it three times, to let them know Victor's okay," Michelle commented as they plodded along.

"You're right," Stacey agreed. "Mish—you go ahead and tell them we're coming."

"You're sure? You don't need me?" Michelle looked anxiously at her, but Stacey shook her head. "Well—okay then. I'll hurry," Michelle added, and cantered off in a scuffle of dust.

The Bend was quiet, its small animals keeping cool underground. The gray-green sage, black branches of greasewood and mesquite, yellow flowers of rabbit brush —all hung motionless in silence broken only by the plop of footsteps, jingle of the bridle, and Victor's occasional sneeze. The hills were so far, the Bend such a monotonous spread of rocks and gray-green shrubs, that Stacey felt as if she were moving through a dream. It's like treading water, only we're on a horse, she thought.

After what seemed like a long time, they heard a shot. "That's for you," Stacey said. "Michelle must have told them, so they're letting the searchers know you're found. Let's count. There's the second—and the third. Three shots mean you're safe." And alive, she thought, but she didn't say that.

Victor sat up straighter. "They're shooting guns? What for?"

"Because people are all over the mountains looking for you. Some have walkie-talkies, but most of them don't."

"Sort of a code?"

"Sort of."

Some time later they heard a faint shout and saw a billow of dust, and as it came closer, Stacey realized that it was stirred up by Fritz on one of the camp horses, Michelle on Tommy Rot, and a stranger on Jeff's own Cherokee, riding awkwardly with his elbows bobbing and toes turned out. When they reached Stacey and Victor, they pulled to an abrupt stop, and the stranger slid to the ground.

"Victor!" He limped forward, a tall man, very thin, with dark-rimmed glasses.

Victor clutched Stacey. "It's my dad!" he whispered. "Something happened to his leg!"

The stranger wrapped both long arms around Victor's waist and gave him a hug. "Fella! Are you all right?"

"Sure," Victor muttered, rigid against Stacey. "I just found me a real neat canyon and stayed there awhile."

"Good for you!" his father was still holding Victor fast. "You had us scared."

Victor pressed his head against Stacey's back. "Are you—pretty mad?" he asked, barely above a whisper.

"Well—you managed to stir up a peck of trouble. But I'm mostly glad you're found."

"I guess I was dumb. About the barn."

Fritz, still on his horse, gave him a grim smile. "It wasn't your best move. But no lives were lost."

"Stacey already told me that."

"And Victor. . . ." His father hesitated. "The boy you were with . . . Sam, I think . . . explained that he persuaded you to take him up there, and that he was the one who lighted the match."

"Stupe!" muttered Michelle.

By now Victor had relaxed his grip on Stacey's waist and was facing his father. "Suppose we both move onto my horse and give this one a rest," the tall man told him, holding out his hands. "We McCauleys ought to stick together."

"Okay. Here I come." Victor slid off Whisper's back, and a few minutes later they were all jogging toward camp, with father and son on Cherokee, Fritz beside them, and the two girls following along.

"Do you care to tell me what happened?" Victor's father asked.

This time Victor was ready to explain. "I was trying to show Sam the hay, but my flashlight went out."

"So that's it!" Stacey exclaimed. "Victor, why wouldn't you tell me?"

"I'm not a rat," the child announced with dignity, glancing back at her. "I never squeal."

"And who was the other boy? Sam?"

"Sam Westlund. He's cool."

"Your first friend at camp," Fritz reminded him. "We're glad you have a buddy, Victor. But no more sneaking out." He guided his horse closer to Cherokee, and his voice softened. "Your dad is quite a cowboy."

"Cowboy?"

"Sure. He's been out in the mountains with me ever since he came, which was pretty fast, soon as we telephoned that you were lost." Fritz began to grin. "I don't think he's had much experience with horses."

"Is that how you hurt your leg?"

Victor's father made a wry face. "Fell off."

"But he climbed back on," Fritz explained. "No little thing like a sprained knee would stop him."

"And I picked up more than a sprain on that jaunt," said the tall man, rubbing his knee. "Fritz and I had a good talk. I understand some things quite a lot better now —such as how it feels to be dumped into a strange camp, when your mom's sick."

"I'll say," muttered Michelle, but she was silenced by Stacey.

"Is Mommy getting better?" asked Victor in an odd, tight little voice.

"Lots better." His father sighed. "Victor, can you understand that sometimes grown-ups get all mixed up? Have more than they can handle? That's why I sent you to camp—I thought you'd have kids to play with and something to do while Mommy got well. But now I realize—well, it wasn't the place for you after all."

"M-m-m. . . ." Victor seemed to be thinking. "It's a good *camp*, all right, if you like camps. Only . . . home is . . . home. . . ." He brushed a wrist across his eyes.

"You want to go home?"

Victor nodded.

"Today, maybe?"

"If I . . . *could* we? This very day?"

"Soon as you can get packed."

"*Well*. . . ." Victor drew a long breath. "That won't take much time at all. I'm a real fast packer. I'll do it just as soon as we get back to camp." He began to chatter about when they could start and how glad his mother would be to see him.

"I'll miss you, Victor," Stacey called, when he ran down. And I really mean it! she thought with surprise.

"That's all right," he called back. "I'll ask my dad to bring me to your ranch sometime, so I can see how Breeze is getting along. I expect he'll grow up pretty fast."

"I expect he will."

With Victor happily planning his trip home, Stacey was free to think. She wondered about Victor's father, who had shipped his son to camp to get him out of the way, and who hadn't even come for Parents' Day. She'd been sure he was a heel—but how about the tender way he had folded Victor in his arms, and his determination to keep searching, even after he fell off the horse? Was he kind after all, even if he didn't figure things out very well?

She thought about Rod Wright—a rancher, and most ranchers were good. But Rod . . . well, as Mish said, Rod stank.

About Fritz and Penny, leaders of the obnoxious camp—and they were fun.

About Tiny, tough cowhand—who wrote poems.

And then the *thing* began to needle her again. Although she was determined to find the key this time, her mind was blank. She tried to trick it. She pretended she didn't want to remember. She told herself it didn't matter. When that didn't work, she concentrated on how important it was.

There must be *some* way to figure it out. Was it about a horse? She named them over: Whisper, Tommy Rot, Breeze, Lady Jane. A person? She thought about people: her family, Tiny, Gwen, Victor, Fritz. She thought about what she liked best: riding and picnics and reading a good book. Nothing helped.

Although Fritz and Victor were talking again, Stacey didn't pay much attention until Victor called back to her. "What's that word, Stacey? Pecko—Peckig—"

"Petroglyphs," she replied.

"That's right. Pet-ro-glyphs. They're neat. I rubbed some."

"Rubbed them? Well—" his father said. "What are they like, anyway?"

"Oh—little men," Stacey told him. "Devil signs. Antelope. Birds. Sort of stick figures that. . . ." She broke off, because the *thing* had come to her all at once, as if a curtain had gone up on a stage. That was it! It had to be!

"Fritz—do you mind if I—if Mish and I—if we go on ahead?" Her words were falling all over each other. "We've got something to do."

"Sure. We can manage. But, Stacey. . . ." Fritz frowned. "Have you had too much sun? You've turned red as a strawberry shortcake."

"I'm all right! Better than you could guess!" She

rode closer to Michelle. "Come along! I want you to help me!"

"Well—crimeny!" exclaimed Michelle. "Can't we get Victor home first?"

"Come *on!*"

"I want to see what everybody says. It'll be a regular celebration."

"There'll be a celebration, all right, if this works."

"If what works?"

"I'll tell you soon enough. But I'm going right now, and if you miss it, you'll be sorry."

"Well—okay. Only I think you're nuts."

"Maybe I am!" Stacey dug her knees into Whisper's sides. "And then again, maybe not. I'll see you later, Victor. Bye for now."

"Bye!" His voice floated after her as she nudged Whisper into a gallop and started for home.

14.
Michelle Talks
Too Much

Mish didn't mean to do it,
of course. But she really
pulled a dumb-dumb trick.
—STACEY'S DIARY
JULY 25

STACEY KEPT WHISPER at a fast canter, swerving around rocks and brush.

"Hey! I'm back here!" Michelle shouted. "And Tommy—!" She broke off as he made a flying leap over a small clump of sage.

"Oh—sorry." Stacey slowed down.

"What is this, anyway?" Michelle's voice was coming in joggles.

"Never mind. I'll tell you when we get there." Going

176

at a pace Tommy could match, Stacey left the Bend and made a wide circle around the camp. She didn't want any excited kids to stop them now.

They walked their horses up the knoll and pulled to a halt beside the kitchen door. "C'mon!" Stacey exclaimed, as she flung herself off Whisper's back. "Two can work faster than I could alone."

Michelle folded her arms and set her chin. "First you have to explain."

"I will. Upstairs."

"Aren't we going to put Whisper and Tommy into the pasture? You know what Dad says—take care of your animals first. They can't do it for themselves."

"We'll give them water, and we've already walked them cool. They can stand here for a little while, and—Mish! It's important. It may save our land. And. . . ."

Michelle slid to the ground. "Save the land? You mean, stop that puky Rod Wright?"

"Maybe."

"Well, why didn't you say so in the first place? Let's get going."

They watered the horses and tied them to a railing in the backyard, where ropes were always ready. "It shouldn't take very long," Stacey said, halfway up the attic stairs.

At the top the air was hot, dry, and dusty, with its own peculiar smell of time long gone. "Now. . . ." Stacey flung open the door. "Gwen and I found some letters and journals that belonged to Grandmother Lucy, and they were full of little pictures."

"So . . . she drew lots of scenery—mountains, lakes, flowers. I think I saw some petroglyphs too, and *maybe* one was a bird with a broken wing. But I hardly looked, because I didn't know it mattered."

"She drew that very glyph? Wow!"

"*Maybe* she did and maybe not. And I don't know what she said—if she drew it. But I *think*, while we were looking for Victor, I saw a glyph in a canyon, just like the one she drew, and it's away out on the Bend. So, if Rod Wright is trying to pull a trick. . . ."

"Well, for cripe's sake, hurry up!"

"I'm trying. Here, give me a hand." Stacey was already tugging at Lucy's trunk, and now, with the help of Michelle, she scraped it across the wooden floor to the window and lifted the lid.

"Lucy's wedding bouquet. But it doesn't smell of flowers anymore. Just old," she said, as she began to sort through the contents of the upper tray. "It isn't in an account book or a letter. I'm pretty sure of that. We want her journals." She flipped through several books and laid three of them aside. "Here they are. Want to try one?"

"Sure. What do I look for?"

"A petroglyph. Don't read the whole thing, just glance through, sort of like when we helped Dad in the

courthouse. See if she said anything about petroglyphs—
or drew some."

"I get it."

With Michelle settled, Stacey sat on the floor, leaned
against the little trunk, and opened a journal. She found a
sketch of a rearing horse, with an entry about a neighbor
who had traded one off; a bearded man wielding a club over
someone who lay at his feet, with Lucy's tale of a young
farmer whose skull had been "cracked" in a brawl; a soldier
carrying a marvelously lengthened gun, with an account of
a cousin who had gone to fight in the War Between the
States. She only scanned them, working fast.

"Hey! These are really good!" Michelle said, looking
up from the other book. "Lots better than those old
deeds."

"I know."

The attic was hot. A fly droned against a window; the
crisp, old paper crackled. Stacey had almost finished the
first journal and was beginning to think that maybe she
hadn't remembered it after all, but only hoped.

And suddenly she stiffened. There they were—tiny
drawings on a cliff: an antelope; a curled-up "water devil";
the sun; and a pair of fighting birds, one of which had a
wing that bent down, as if it had been broken. All of them
were strewn on the cliff, helter-skelter, as if someone had
doodled them there.

But, oh!—most important!—instead of showing
every figure "high overhead," the drawing placed most of

them at the level of a man and woman who were standing close by. Only the sun was high, and it was a peculiar sun, because its rays were not straight, but bent.

"Mish!" Stacey turned it so her sister could see. "This is what kept bothering me! I saw it up here before, and forgot it! But I had it on the inside somewhere, telling me that Rod was all wrong!"

"You remembered it? Sort of?" Michelle seemed puzzled.

"*No!* I told you, I *forgot* it! I just had a scratchy feeling." Stacey paused, thinking about their search on the Bend. "And Mish—the best part! In one of those canyons—today—I saw a sun just like this. With those squiggly rays. All by itself, high up. At least I think so. Only I don't know whether the other glyphs are there or not, because I didn't look."

She held the journal up for better light. "Hear what Lucy says: '*Charles showed me some of the boundaries of the ranch—he's had the deed filed now, so it's really ours. And it's so romantic! Our eastern line runs from an Indian carving—a muddle of darling little sketches—in the seventh canyon of the Bend. Mr. Severne, the surveyor, drove the pipes, at the foot of "our" pictures, while we were there. A wonderful marker. And a wonderful, happy day.*' "

Stacey glanced at Michelle. "Do you see what that means? It means that the one Rod Wright showed us is probably wrong, because *all* the parts of his petroglyph are 'high above.' But Lucy says, plain as day, 'at the foot of our pictures,' and she drew only the sun high up, and with those funny rays. Now," Stacey started to put the journals and books into their place in the trunk, "if I can find that sun again—and if the other glyphs are there, too —then the pipes must be on the canyon floor, and that would clinch it. Let's go look."

"Well, crumb-bum! Sure!" Michelle scrambled to her feet.

"We'll have to take rags so we can mark it!" Stacey exclaimed as they shoved the trunk back under the eaves.

"My old bandanna. It's almost a rag already."

"Good!" They raced down the stairs.

They were soon on their way. "Seventh canyon. That must be pretty far. And for cripe's sake, how many are there?" Michelle asked, as they jogged along. Tommy was going well, bobbing his head, waggling his ears. "Did she count all the gullies, or just the big ones? Are you sure you saw that squiggly sun?"

"I'm not sure of anything," Stacey replied, almost crossly. "How could I be!"

They passed the gentle slope that led into the first ravine. "It's farther than this. I know that much," Stacey remarked.

At the next they stopped to let their horses rest while they peered over the rocky ledge to the bottom, where a silver shine marked the course of a stream. "Puma Creek," Michelle remarked. "But I never saw a puma there, did you?"

"Never," Stacey agreed. "But we're still too near the house. Are you ready? Has Tommy had enough rest?"

"I guess," Michelle replied, and they started again.

Now the ravines were closer together, some steep, some gradual, and the girls decided they were far enough into the Bend to begin their search. After tearing the bandanna in half so they could each have some, they started to ride down the slopes and along the bottoms as far as they could, then out to the Bend again. They searched one, and another, and another.

"It's hard to know where Lucy's path went," Stacey said. "And anyway, I've lost count. Is this number seven?"

"Or eight? Or six—or ten?"

"I couldn't even guess. But it seems like the one where I saw that sun. The rocks were about this high." Stacey held Whisper firmly, helping her down the steep path to the creek, where they let their horses have a drink, then separated, because the canyon branched.

Stacey moved slowly along, tilting back her head until her neck ached, scanning every rock that loomed above the brush. She mustn't miss anything, because something about this place—the height of the walls, per-haps—made her feel hopeful. Any minute—any *second* now—she might find the place. It might be just around that rock. Or the next.

And *what was that?* Above that thicket? A carving! Yes! The squiggly sun! *High overhead!* "That's it!" she screamed, so suddenly that Whisper tossed her head and snorted. "Sorry, girl. It's all right." She rode the horse as close as she could, slid off, and dropped her reins.

She'd fought her way through a thicket exactly like this when she was looking for Victor. She remembered scrambling over some branches and stooping under some, just as she was doing now. When she'd reached the rock wall, there'd been a clear space, almost like the one where they'd finally found him, but she'd been looking for a boy, not rocks, so she had only a vague idea of the carvings.

But today she'd look—*and there they were!* The fighting birds with the broken wing! The antelope! The devil marks! And only the sun was high! The rest were close to the ground, exactly as in Lucy's picture.

After checking every element, Stacey looked on the canyon floor for pipes, but found none. Thinking that they were probably buried by now, she decided not to waste time in a search, and scrambled back through the brush to Whisper, who was nibbling a patch of bunch grass. She tied a strip of bandanna to a chest-high bush, mounted, and started up the canyon at a trot.

"Mish! Mish! Come quick! I found it!"

In a few minutes she met her sister, riding pell-mell. "It's here? It really *is?*" Michelle shouted. "Well— grapes! Show me!" They rode back to the thicket, and Michelle went inside for a look. "The pipes?" she asked.

"I can't find any," Stacey told her. "But they might be hidden under the brush."

Afterward, when they had returned to the upper

level of the Bend and fastened another strip of bandanna to the canyon entrance, Stacey insisted that nothing was certain yet. "We'll have to get Dad and Mar to have a look, and I suppose a surveyor, too."

"Let's hurry up." Michelle gave Tommy a kick, and they were off.

They rode fast, not talking, and were about halfway home when Michelle pulled Tommy to a halt. "Stace! Look! That *creep!* Do we *have* to talk to him?" She pointed ahead to Rod Wright, who was driving his Jeep toward them.

"Not unless he sees us," Stacey cheerfully assured her. Even Rod couldn't upset her today. "Try turning right."

Rod, however, had spotted them. When they turned, he did too, and in a few minutes he stopped his Jeep in front of them.

"Afternoon!" he affably remarked, climbing out and wiping his forehead. "Another scorcher."

"Yes. But it's always like this—or almost always—in July," Stacey replied, trying not to let her triumph show.

"To be sure. To be sure. I hear you had a bit of excitement over your way. Just came to make sure everything is all right. I feel—well—considerable concern these days, about anything that happens at the camp."

"Yes. It was exciting. But it's all right now," Stacey replied.

"Good! Good!"

Michelle's face was scarlet. "You don't need to feel concerned about the camp! Not anymore!" she blurted. "It isn't yours!"

"Not as yet," he blandly agreed, as he pulled out a package and started to offer it to them, then held it back. "You don't like gum, do you? I remember that well. Always try to keep those little details in mind." He popped two sticks into his mouth. "Now, about the fire. Since I'll soon. . . ."

"You'll soon!" Michelle thrust out her chin. "You won't soon be doing anything, that's what you won't! Because we've found the real petroglyph! In a canyon! And we've marked it with. . . ."

"Mish!" Stacey interrupted. "That's enough!"

Michelle shrank into her saddle, glowering.

"Mr. Wright," Stacey continued, "we really have to get home. And you mustn't pay any attention to Michelle. She . . . she gets kind of excited sometimes. It's nothing to worry about."

"Worry? Oh, I won't worry!" Rod replied with a beaming smile. "I never feel it pays to worry." He climbed back into his Jeep and started its engine. "Goodbye now. You've evidently had—quite a day." Giving them a friendly wave, he roared off in the direction they had come.

A few minutes later, when Stacey looked back, his Jeep was already out of sight, leaving a trail of dust.

15.
What Happened
in the Canyon

I didn't think even Rod Wright
would be that low.

—STACEY'S DIARY

JULY 25

STACEY KEPT WHISPER at a swift canter over the Bend, not trying to hold her back, even for the sake of little Tommy Rot. She felt that in exactly one more second she would explode. Couldn't Mish—*ever*—have enough sense to hold her tongue? Bragging to Rod Wright! Telling him what they'd found! *Where was he going so fast in that Jeep?*

Michelle didn't seem to realize what she'd done. "He's *awful!*" she shouted as Tommy pounded along, doing his gallant best to keep up. "He—he *stinks!*"

"He does," Stacey shouted back, "and *you stink, too.* Why can't you learn to *keep your big, fat mouth shut!*"

Michelle's reply was high and sharp. "So what have I done now, Miss Biggety? Always telling me, *'Michelle, do this! Michelle, do that! Michelle, you've made another boo-boo!'* Well—I'm getting tired of having you tell me about my boo-boos, that's what. You make a few yourself sometimes. You. . . ."

"*Oh!*" Stacey gave Whisper a nudge that sent her even faster. "You told Rod Wright what we've found. That we'd marked it. That's all. He'll see our rags, right off. So now. . . ."

Tommy Rot was dropping behind. "Cri-i-ipes!" wailed Michelle. "Stace—I never thought. . . ."

"As usual." Stacey also slowed down, thinking that Michelle might be a toad, but even so, they shouldn't abuse her pony. For that matter, there was no point in having a real fight. "Oh, well—it's done," she said. "So now let's figure out what next, like getting Mar or Dad."

Michelle thumped her own head with her fist. "I'm *sorry*, Stace. I'm always having to be sorry for something. It's just like you said. I open my big, fat mouth, and there's no telling what will come out. But you're right. We'd better get help."

"Yes. Fast." Stacey nudged Whisper and they were off again, hot air flowing past her face, Whisper rocking beneath her. They skirted a gnarled green juniper and dodged a ball of tumbleweed. Mar or Dad would know what to do.

But when the girls reached the house, it was silent.

"Mar?" Michelle called, pounding through the rooms. No answer.

"Dad?" Stacey poked her head out of the back door and shouted. "Hey—somebody!" There was no reply. Jeff, she knew, would be busy at the camp, but Mar— could she have gone to work so soon after the fire? And Dad—?

Hearing some loud bangs, she ran outside, followed by Michelle, and found Tiny in the tractor shed, with a hammer and chain saw and a stack of boards.

"Fixing up a stall for the foals," he explained. "So we can get them under shelter if it storms."

"Where's Dad?" the girls asked, both at once.

Tiny set down the hammer. "Gone to town, to see about insurance."

"And Mar—?"

"Him and your mother both. They've got to rebuild the barn—buy some feed—buy new tack. Big job, a fire is."

"I know it. But Tiny, we *need* them."

"And they might be gone for *hours,*" said Michelle.

"Yes. So . . . so. . . ." Stacey could think of only one solution. "Tiny, *you* come with us. Rod Wright's on his way."

"And he's *awful!*" exclaimed Michelle.

Stacey caught her breath. "I'll get Mar's camera, and take a picture. Then we'll at least have a record of. . . ."

"Who-o-oa!" Tiny exclaimed. "You're ten miles ahead of me. What in thunderation has got you into such a state?"

"It's mostly my fault," Mish said, while Stacey tried at the same time to tell him where they'd been.

"Now—easy!" Tiny held up his hand. "I've got two ears, but they only work as a team. You'll have to drive past them one at a time."

As calmly as she could, with Michelle nodding and gasping beside her, Stacey related what had happened. "So, please come. If Rod's there—well, I'd like to have somebody to. . . ."

"M-m-m! That fellow! Never did trust him, and it's too bad. His dad was a mighty good neighbor." Tiny was already at the door of the shed. "Always carry a bridle in my car. I'll get it and catch Sultan, while you, Stacey, dig up that camera. Good idea, making a record. Right away."

"Oh, Tiny—*thank* you," Stacey said, but Tiny was gone.

"Mish," Stacey continued, "I'll go with Tiny, while you get hold of Mar and Dad. Phone the insurance office. It's the Ranchers' Life, or something like that. If they aren't there, get somebody to look for them. Figure out something. Go to the Double Star if you have to and ask Gwen's mom to take you to town."

They were running up the knoll to the house. "I'll find them," Michelle said. "Don't worry. I will."

"If you go to Gwen's, take Nutmeg. She's faster than Tommy. Can you catch her?"

"Don't be a clod!"

A few minutes later, when Stacey was ready to leave the house, she heard Michelle on the telephone. "It's *really important.* I absolutely *have* to talk to. . . ."

Stacey didn't wait for the rest. Mish would manage.

She found Tiny beside the back door, long legs wrapped around Sultan's massive body. "Now, let's have it again," he said as soon as they were on their way toward the Bend. "You say Rod Wright's trying to put over a fast one?"

"I think so. Dad told us that nobody ever checked the boundary line, because the land's so poor. And now the surveyors can't find the pipes—but they're looking on the upper level of the Bend instead of on the floor. And *our* petroglyph is just right. And Lucy's journal. . . ."

Tiny interrupted. "It's still all of a muddle to me, and this isn't the time to straighten it out. That fellow Wright. . . ." His voice turned deep:

" 'A man designed for perfidy, for crime,
We'll keep him in our eye.' "

He clucked to Sultan. "Just let's get there and take your pictures."

The wind had set the sagebrush to quivering, and a dust devil whirled across their path. As Stacey rode swiftly along, she could hear Sultan's heavy hoofbeats just behind, the most comforting sound in the world, she thought, because it meant that Tiny would be there to help her if she met Rod Wright.

They swiftly passed one canyon after another, until she saw the red bandanna, lifting and falling in the breeze. There, with Tiny close behind, she started down.

At the bottom all was still. No birds were singing. No small animals scampered across their path. They heard only the crunch of dried twigs under the hoofs, an occasional snuffle from their horses, and the hiss of dust blown along close to the ground.

But in a few minutes Tiny, who was riding ahead, stopped and raised his hand. "Unless my ears are playing me tricks, somebody's up ahead," he said in a husky undertone.

Stacey pulled to a stop, and—yes. She heard it, too. "Sort of a thumping sound? Could it be a deer?"

"It's no deer, and I don't like it," Tiny replied. He pulled back on Sultan, who was pawing the ground. "Stacey, I'm right glad you brought that camera. Sure you can work it?"

"Mar taught me how."

"Good." He slid off Sultan's back. "We'll lead our horses in, quiet as we can, and find out what's up."

As they worked their way along, the sound became louder, a crunching, rhythmic *k'chunk*—pause—*k'chunk*.

When they reached the thicket where Stacey had tied the bandanna, the sound was close, coming from behind the brush.

Finger to his lips, Tiny dropped reins, and Stacey did the same, following him into the center. And there was Rod Wright, with his back to them, vigorously swinging a sledge hammer at the rock wall—the wall of the petroglyphs.

With every swing he swayed back and forth on his enormous feet, and he was puffing too hard to hear them come. When Tiny stopped and motioned to Stacey, she opened Mar's camera and took a picture, a good one, she thought, showing Rod's back, the uplifted mallet, and most of the glyph.

Tiny pointed to a closer spot, and she tiptoed forward for another shot. He motioned again, and she moved to the side, to catch Rod's face. But this time she stepped on a dry twig with a snap that made him turn around—and she had the best picture of all.

Rod snarled, "Turning photographer, my dear?"

"I think she's caught you, fair and square," Tiny told him in an angry rumble. "And it looks as if we're just in time." He pointed to the cliff, where the smallest antelope had been almost chipped away.

Carefully Rod set his mallet on the ground. "A schoolgirl picture?" he mocked. "What, please, has she 'caught'—as you put it?"

"Most likely a rat." Tiny drew a deep breath, and his bony frame seemed to swell. " 'Seek not to deny your own foul perfidy, but craven slink away!' " He sucked in another breath. " 'There be land-rats and water-rats, land-thieves and water-thieves.' "

"Thieves!" Rod stared at Stacey and her camera, then folded his arms and seemed to shrink as if air were escaping from a balloon. "Let's not be hasty. After all, we're friends." He rearranged his scowl into a beaming smile. "I'd never stoop to thievery. I—that is—the girls said they'd found these petroglyphs, and . . . I thought they might be important. So I brought some tools. Thought I'd just clear away the brush." He swept his hand toward a chopped-off branch. "To make it more accessible. You can understand that."

"I understand, all right. You and your schemes!" Stacey burst out. "You can bang away all you want to now. I've got three pictures that will make my dad really happy!" *Wow!* she thought. *A regular Mish-explosion, and it felt good!*

Rod picked up his mallet. "Sure . . . sure. Didn't mean harm to anyone. It's not my way to quarrel with a neighbor." His smile was, if possible, even wider than before. "I'll be right glad to see your daddy, any time he wants. We can work this thing out. . . ."

"Well, I'm going straight home. Just remember, this canyon belongs to the Rocking C," Stacey replied.

"That's right. So you—*git!*" added Tiny, stepping aside and standing motionless with his arms folded, while Rod lumbered out of the thicket and away.

When they were halfway home, Tiny and Stacey were met by Michelle, who was pounding along on Nutmeg, her face red and braids bouncing. "Did you get some pictures?" she shouted when she was still so far they could barely hear. "Hey! Did you?" Coming close, she pulled up beside them. "Do you think that glyph is a good one, Tiny?"

"Good enough to trip up friend Wright." Grinning, Tiny drew to a halt.

"Did you find Dad? Or Mar?" Stacey demanded.

"Both!" Michelle happily replied. "The insurance man went after them, and they're coming home straight off. We'd better hurry back, or they'll beat us there." She turned Nutmeg around, and they rode back together through the brilliant sunset, red and purple and gold, with the Bend lying dark around them.

The following evening Stacey and Mar, Tiny and Michelle gathered for dinner—hot dogs and doughnuts, because it was Mish's turn to cook. They had almost finished when Jeff and their father came in beaming and dropped down at the table.

"Did you find anything?" asked Mar.

Dad's grin broadened. "I'll say we did. The pipes. At the bottom of the canyon, just as Grandmother Lucy's journal said. No wonder the surveyors drew a blank—they were running metal detectors all over the Bend. On top."

"Lucy was quite a girl!" said Jeff, as he poured out a glob of catsup.

"We called on Rod, too," their father continued. "He's withdrawing his claim. Put up a long story. . . ."

"He's a whiner," added Jeff.

"Right. And a coward. Grabbing at the easy way."

"How could anybody try to cheat a *neighbor!*" said Stacey. "Even him. . . ."

"I don't think he started out to cheat us," Mar said. "When he checked the deed and remembered the glyph —and found it—he must have been excited. And for a while he actually believed the land was his."

"Right," their father agreed. "Having, as he thought, 'owned' it for a few weeks, he got to counting on it. And when you kids told him you'd found the true monument, he couldn't bear to give it up. So. . . ."

"So a rancher tried to steal our land!" Stacey exclaimed. "Everything's backwards. Penny and Fritz are nice. Pathetic little darling Victor broke his promises."

"You can't count on anybody," Michelle broke in. "That Myrna—she stayed for this session too, like Victor, only she wanted to. Well, all last term she was my best friend down there. Anyway I thought so. But now with those new kids, when they chose up tent partners for the campout, she . . . she. . . ." Michelle swelled with indignation. *"She's teamed off with somebody else."*

"There must be other nice girls for you to be chums with," Mar said serenely.

"Oh, sure. I've already got Wendy. She wants to raise worms, like me."

Tiny, who had been keeping his eyes fixed on his plate, reached his fork across the table and speared a doughnut.

> " 'The fault was Nature's fault not thine,
> Which made thee fickle as thou art.' "

He broke the doughnut in half. "You're doing just right, Michelle. Keep your rope coiled, ready for the next throw."

After a moment's silence Michelle spoke again. "Stace—I almost forgot. Penny asked me to tell you something. Well . . . she didn't really ask me to, but she said. . . . Anyway, I was telling them about our glyphs . . ."

"Naturally." Stacey reflected that she could count on Mish, at least. She'd always be the same little blabbermouth.

"And they thought it was super-exciting. And so did some of the kids. . . ."

"I suppose you told them a good story, too."

Michelle seemed oblivious to the irony. "Well— pretty good," she said. "Anyway, Penny thinks that mak-

ing some rubbings would be a really neat field trip. And
Fritz thinks so, too. Only they'd need some help
to. . . ."

Almost as if she were standing in the middle of it,
Stacey saw the camp, with Penny and Fritz smiling on the
front steps, and the kids laughing in the lake.

"They told me that before," she said. "Actually, I've
been thinking about it." She folded her napkin, laid
it carefully beside her plate, and stalked out the door.
Nobody spoke, and in the silence she could feel their
eyes upon her. Let them stare, she told herself. She had
a right to change her mind if she wanted to. And a right
to think.

Outside, the sky was a close, warm black, with stars
like lamps. A tender breeze from the mountains lifted the
ends of Stacey's hair; and down below, reflected in a long,
ruddy streak across the lake, she could see the glow of a
campfire. Locusts were chirring; a horse nickered; and
faintly, carried on the breeze, she could hear a song—the
melody only, but she knew the words.

"Tell me why the sky's so blue.
Tell me, Rocking C, why we love you."

They loved Rocking C! Just as she did! The campers
weren't anything like she'd expected. They didn't bother
anybody much, and they did lots of interesting things.
Like that basketry class. And the painting class. And
petroglyphs. What did the art teacher do with those?

The song died away, but another began, as familiar as the first.

> "I've got the whole wide world
> In my hands."

As Stacey listened, her resentment seemed to turn into a hard ball and roll away, leaving her with a new, free, light feeling. She guessed it was time to take another look at a lot of people. It didn't work to make up your mind about anybody until you'd found out what they were really like. You ought to get acquainted first, and then decide.

The campers were still singing, and their fire seemed brighter now. Something special always happened at the campfires, or so Michelle had said. If she hurried, she'd be there in time. She'd just sit at the edge tonight and listen, but tomorrow she'd offer to show them some glyphs that would make really good rubbings. The antelope, or maybe the water-devil. She'd plan a nice overnight for them, too, probably to High Tor, the best ride of all. She'd lead the way—she and Whisper—and Michelle could ride along, if she wanted to.

Humming the campers' song, she started down the knoll.